He was not a man to cross

"There is no law on Isla de la Pantera except my law," Roarke said harshly. "Everything on this island is my property."

"Not me," she said quickly. "Not—"

"Everything," he repeated, and his mouth dropped to hers. His hands slipped up her throat to her face, framing it so that she couldn't escape the kiss no matter how desperately she struggled.

"You can't fight me," he whispered, drawing back a little, enough so that she could see the darkness in his eyes. "Do you understand?"

"I hate you," she gritted.

SANDRA MARTON says she has always believed in the magic of storytelling and the joy of living happily ever after with that special someone. She wrote her first romance story when she was nine, seven years before she fell madly in love with the man she would eventually marry. Today, after raising two sons and an assortment of four-legged creatures, Sandra and her husband live in a house on a hilltop in a quiet corner of Connecticut.

Books by Sandra Marton

SANDRA MARTON

Roarke's Kingdom

Harlequin Books

TORONTO • NEW YORK • LONDON
AMSTERDAM • PARIS • SYDNEY • HAMBURG
STOCKHOLM • ATHENS • TOKYO • MILAN
MADRID • WARSAW • BUDAPEST • AUCKLAND

Harlequin Presents first edition July 1993
ISBN 0-373-11574-1

Original hardcover edition published in 1991
by Mills & Boon Limited

ROARKE'S KINGDOM

PROLOGUE

HE ROSE from the aquamarine sea in a burst of shimmering radiance. Water streamed from his golden body, drops glittering like tiny stars in the dark hair that thatched his muscled chest and arrowed down his flat belly into his narrow Spandex swimsuit.

The tropical sun was hot on his skin, as warm as a woman's caress. Slowly, deliberately, he lifted his face to it, eyes closed against the white-hot glare, willing himself to let go the accumulated tensions of the working week.

After a while he felt his muscles begin to loosen and relax. The combination of sea and sun was an irresistible panacea, but it was not the reason why he came to this primitive place time and time again.

He came because there were no intrusions, no harsh reminders of the world that he commanded. Here, no one scurried to do his bidding, no hypocrites smiled at his every joke or hung on his words with an almost palpable obsequiousness.

The silence of this timeless place was a potent luxury. Only the boom and hiss of the surf as it beat against the white sand crescent that marked the seaward perimeter of his island reached his ears. There were no other sounds. No growling powerboats, no blaring radios, no flickering television screens. Necessity had dictated the installation of a telephone, but the few people entrusted with its number knew better than to use it except in matters of grave urgency.

This place, this tiny outcropping of rock, sand, and palms that rose from the Caribbean just off the coast of Puerto Rico, was Roarke Campbell's private domain. It was his, and his alone, and it had no rules but those he wished.

Making the island his had not been easy, but then, he had not expected it to be.

"*Sí, señor,* we understand that you wish to buy Isla de la Pantera," each successive government official had said patiently. "But it is not for sale."

Of course, in the end, it had been. Things always were—for a price. If there had been one great lesson in Roarke's life, it was that. You could buy anything, if you had enough money.

"Señor Campbell?"

Roarke blinked and turned toward the shore. For a moment, the light dazzled him, and he shaded his eyes with his hands. A slow smile angled across his face when he saw the woman standing on the sand, a squirming child in her arms.

"Your daughter is awake," she said in Spanish. "I told her that her *Papá* was here, but she wanted to be certain."

His smile broadened, softening the harsh planes and angles of his face, and he trotted quickly to the beach. The child laughed with joy as she went eagerly into his open arms.

"Daddy here," she said, and Roarke's arms tightened around her.

"Always," he said, and for an instant the dark intensity was back in his eyes. "Always, sweetheart."

The little girl squealed happily as he hoisted her on to his shoulders. A bittersweet joy rose within him as her hands clutched at his dark, wet hair.

How could he have forgotten? There *was* something money couldn't buy...

The love of this child.

His daughter.

Roarke's smile fled. Any other kind of love was as much for sale as Isla de la Pantera.

He knew that first hand. It was a lesson he had learned well.

CHAPTER ONE

VICTORIA'S flight lifted into the Chicago sky just as a midwinter storm swept in from Canada. She had a last glimpse of a world turned white by snow, and then thick clouds rolled across her window. Everything turned gray, as if a giant hand had suddenly wrapped the DC-10 in cotton batting.

A woman in the seat across from hers laughed nervously as the plane was swallowed up in the weather. "What a day for flying," she said to nobody in particular.

Victoria knotted her hands together in her lap. And what a day for your first ever flight, she thought. But at least the plane had got away. There'd been delay after delay while the weather built up, until finally the only thing that had seemed more frightening than the lowering sky was the possibility that the flight to San Juan might be canceled.

"It's really rotten out there, isn't it?"

The pleasant male voice startled her. Victoria looked up as a man eased into the empty aisle seat beside her. He was young, good-looking, and the smile he flashed was filled with equal parts strong white teeth, male assurance, and charm.

Victoria looked at the seatbelt sign, which was still on, and his smile took on a boyish dazzle.

"I know, I know. I should have stayed put until it went off." He settled beside her and bent his head toward hers. "But I saw this vacancy and I thought, here I am and there you are, with thousands of miles ahead of us . . .''

"I know exactly what you thought." Victoria's blue eyes were as cool as her voice. "And I'm afraid you're wasting your time."

The man's smile faltered a little. "Look, I'm not trying to—it's just that it's a long flight, and——''

"Yes. It is." She reached into her bag and took out a paperback novel. "That's why I brought a book along."

He laughed softly. "A book isn't much company. You looked awfully lonely, sitting here all by yourself. That's why I . . .''

He fell silent as Victoria opened her paperback and bent over the first page, her midnight black hair falling forward like a shield around her face. The letters tumbled before her eyes; she might as well have been reading Sanskrit. But she stared at them as if they made sense, and finally her unwelcome visitor muttered something under his breath. She felt the seat shift. When she dared look up, he was gone.

She closed the book and folded her hands over it. Her hands were trembling, which was ridiculous. Her heart was racing, too, and that was even crazier. This was a public place, packed with people, and the man had only been trying for an easy pickup.

She knew all that. But when he'd said she looked lonely, sitting all by herself, she'd suddenly been tumbled back four years and instead of being on an airplane she was sitting inside a Cadillac, parked under the trees at Boulder Hill with Craig Stevens at her side. A shudder raced through her. No, not at her side. He'd been all over her, his hands everywhere on her body, his mouth slippery on hers . . .

"Ladies and gentlemen, this is your Captain speaking. You'll be happy to hear the weather in San Juan is warm and sunny, with the temperature at eighty-three degrees.'' A faint cheer echoed through the cabin. "We've a strong tail wind, which means we should be landing twenty minutes ahead of time, and———"

"Twenty minutes!" Someone laughed in the seat behind Victoria's. "Well, I suppose that's something. You can't sneer at an extra quarter of an hour in the sun, can you?''

An extra quarter of an hour. Victoria took a deep breath, put her head back, and closed her eyes. No, you couldn't sneer at that. Not when you had only one hundred and twenty hours to make your life mean something.

One hundred and twenty hours. Only five days in which to find the child you'd given birth to and never seen again.

When that was facing you, every minute counted.

Four hours later, Victoria stood under the warmth of the tropical sun, blinking her eyes against the glare. It was as if she had stepped from one world into another, and it took a little getting used to.

The travel agent had told her there'd be nothing to adapt to, but she'd been talking about the one-hour time difference and the fact that many islanders spoke English. She hadn't been referring to the languorous heat or to the scent of flowers that seemed to drift on the air despite the taxis and buses fighting their way past the arrivals terminal at Isla Verde.

"You'll love Puerto Rico," the woman had said as she handed over Victoria's airline tickets and hotel voucher. "The beaches, the hotels, the shopping—it's a nonstop party, my dear. I just know you'll have a lovely time."

Victoria had smiled and said yes, she was sure she would. It had been simpler than telling the woman the truth, which was that the last thing she expected of the five days she could afford to spend in Puerto Rico was a lovely time.

She was here to find L.R. Campbell, and she only had a business address and a fuzzy photo to go on. All she could really tell from the photo was that Campbell was middle-aged, with wire-rimmed glasses and thinning hair. He looked as she expected he would: like a respectable, responsible example of fatherhood.

She had no photo of his wife, nor did she have his home address. The man guarded his privacy zealously; as it was, it had taken the private investigator she'd hired three days—three incredibly expensive days—to learn the little he had about L.R. Campbell.

The cost had taken an alarmingly large bite out of Victoria's inheritance. Her mother's medical bills had been staggering, the funeral costs high despite the simplicity of the casket. Settling those accounts had put an enormous dent in what little money she'd got from the life insurance policy and sale of the ramshackle house in which she'd grown up.

And now she was here, in San Juan, with the situation still unresolved. Victoria sighed as she shifted her suitcase from one hand to the other. The private investigator had been more than willing to get all the answers for her.

"Lissen, Miss Winters, you need to know where this guy lives? It's no problem. I can be in San Juan Friday, bright and early, and be back in Chicago Sunday with the info."

"You mean, you have to go there yourself? Don't you have friends? Contacts?"

The man had grinned at her through a cloud of cigarette smoke. "I think maybe you've seen too many movies, Miss Winters. Who would I know in the Caribbean? Besides, you'd only end up paying the guy down there and maybe he'd string it out and give you nothin'. Believe me, it's cheaper if I fly down myself. I'll have everything you need in two, three days at the most. Okay?''

Victoria had done some rapid figuring. The trip would cost a small fortune, when you added up the cost of the investigator's air fare, hotel, and meals. He'd probably need a rental car, too, and, of course, she'd still be paying his per diem. When he finally flew back with Campbell's home address, she'd have to set out on the very same journey herself, with all the same costs, air fare and hotel and all the rest.

''Thank you,'' she'd said, ''but I'll handle it myself.''

''Get the guy's address?'' The detective had laughed. ''Sure. You go ahead. Do that, lady.''

The airport bus pulled to the curb and the doors hissed open. Victoria climbed the steps, found a seat, and hoisted her suitcase onto the rack. The man's words had been condescending, but they hadn't put her off. She knew where Campbell Enterprises was located, she knew what Campbell looked like. How hard would it be to seek out his office, wait until he left at the end of the day, and follow him home?

She stared blindly out of the window as the bus belched a cloud of black exhaust fumes and shouldered its way into traffic.

With a little luck her journey would come to its end soon. She would see, with her own eyes, the man and woman who had adopted her baby, she would see the house they lived in, and assure herself that Dr. Ronald's promises that her daughter would be well-cared for and grow up loved and wanted were true.

She *wanted* to believe it. But, deep in her heart, she never really had. That was why she was here now, to cast out the doubts that haunted her dreams, to see for herself that she had made the right choice.

And if, by some small miracle, she caught a glimpse of her child along the way, she would cherish the moment for the rest of her life.

By the following day, Victoria was desperate. She had misjudged everything, and the hands of the clock were racing away.

She had envisaged Campbell's company as housed in a narrow, pastel-colored building on a winding, palm-lined street. There would be a burnished brass plaque on the door and a long black limousine at the curb and, at the end of the day, L.R. Campbell, with his thinning hair and wire-rimmed spectacles, would step inside the car and be whisked away, with Victoria following discreetly in a taxi.

Reality shattered that illusion. There *were* sleepy little streets in San Juan, but not in Hato Rey, its modern commercial heart—and that was where she found the glass and concrete high-rise building that bore the address the investigator had given her. The only thing that bore any resemblance to what she'd imagined was the brass plaque on the door. "CAMPBELL'S," it said, in raised letters, but with a sinking heart Victoria realized that the whole building—all fifteen storys of it—belonged to the one company.

She took a deep breath. It would make finding one office—that of L.R. Campbell himself—more difficult, but hardly impossible. A glimpse of the man, just enough to imprint his face on her memory, and then she'd hurry back to the street and wait for closing time.

Electronic doors hissed open automatically, and she stepped into a pink marble lobby. There was an information desk opposite the elevator bank, and a polite but implacable security guard. You couldn't get past the lobby floor unless you had an appointment, he told her. There were no exceptions.

Victoria said the first thing that came into her head. "Well, then, how do you apply for a job?"

The guard smiled. A gold tooth flashed in the corner of his mouth. "Ah, that is different, *señorita*. In that case, you must fill out this form."

"And then?"

"And then you take it to the fourth floor, and hand it to the woman at the desk."

Victoria scratched in quick answers to the employment questionnaire, then waved it in the air.

"All done," she said.

The guard's brows rose, but he shrugged and pointed to the elevator. Her heart pounded as she stepped inside and stared at the numbers on the control panel. Which one? she thought. Which one?

The guard leaned toward her. *"El cuarto piso,"* he called. "The fourth floor, *sí*?"

Victoria swallowed. *"Sí.* Yes. I remember."

She hit the button, trying not to look as nervous as she felt. The doors slid shut, and the elevator began to rise.

She knew instinctively that L.R. Campbell's office would not be on the same floor as the personnel office, but she got out at the fourth floor anyway, just in case the guard was watching the lighted elevator panel. There was a desk ahead of her, but the woman seated at it was engrossed in the letter she was typing. Victoria took a deep breath and began striding purposefully down the corridor toward the fire stairs. She was almost there when a voice called after her.

"Señorita. Señorita? A dónde vás?"

She turned slowly. The woman at the reception desk had risen; she was staring at her.

"I——" Victoria hesitated, then held out the employment application. "I was looking for Personnel. The guard said..."

The woman motioned impatiently. "Have you filled everything in? Give it here, then."

There was no choice but to do as she'd been told. Victoria retraced her steps slowly and handed the form to the woman.

"What kind of job were you looking for? Not that it matters—José should have told you, we're not hiring." The woman frowned as she glanced at the application. "You haven't answered most of the questions, *señorita*." She looked up, her eyes dark with suspicion. "Not even here, where it asks for your name."

Victoria smiled nervously as she backed toward the elevator. "Haven't I? Well, it doesn't matter, does it? I mean, if there aren't any openings——"

"Just one moment, *señorita*. I think I would like to ask you some questions."

Victoria's shoulder blades hit the wall. She turned quickly, stepped into the elevator, and pressed the lobby button.

"*Señorita*, wait——"

The doors slid closed. Victoria sagged back against the wall. What a masterful performance that had been! Another moment, and who knew what would have happened? The woman might have called the guard, or even the police. For all she knew, the woman had done just that; they might be waiting for her even now, as the doors hissed open.

"What the hell's going on?"

The man filled the open elevator doorway. That was her first impression; that, and the fact that he was glaring at her as if she had just committed a crime. His voice was cold and harsh, but not as harsh as the taut, angled lines of his face.

"Well? I'm waiting. What kind of game are you trying to pull?"

Victoria drew a breath. "Would you please step aside?"

The bluff didn't work. He put his hands on his hips and glowered at her.

"I asked you a question, lady. And I still haven't got an answer."

He wasn't a policeman, she thought frantically—not unless the police here dropped out of nowhere, not unless they wore suits of dark silk that had been tailored to fit such wide shoulders, or such a lean, powerful body. Security, then. That was his job, corporate security. L.R. Campbell, with his penchant for privacy, would have someone like this at his beck and call.

She lifted her head until her eyes were locked with his. "Is this the way all visitors are treated at Campbell's?"

His eyes narrowed. "You have one minute to come up with an answer," he said softly.

Victoria's throat constricted. He was trying to intimidate her, and he was succeeding. But she couldn't let him know that—not if she were to get out of here without giving herself away.

"And you," she said, "have one minute to step aside and let me pass."

Something glimmered in the black depths of his eyes. "José?" he said, his eyes locked on hers.

Behind him, the guard snapped to attention. *"Sí, señor."*

"What kind of job did the lady ask for?"

"She did not say, *señor*."

A tight smile curved across the man's mouth. "No," he said softly, "she did not. And she did not write down her preferences on the application form, either."

Victoria swallowed. "I—I wasn't sure what was available."

"Ah. I see. So you'd have taken anything, then."

She nodded. "Yes."

Again, that quick smile that was not a smile flashed across his face.

"Typist."

"Yes."

"Or clerk."

"Yes. I——"

His mouth curled. "Or cleaning woman."

Victoria flushed. "Look, I don't know what this is all about, but——"

"Don't you?"

She shook her head. "No. Just because your employer is paranoid when it comes to privacy——"

It was the wrong thing to say, she knew it as soon as the words left her mouth. The man's eyes flashed with fire. He stepped forward and she fell back into the elevator. The door slid shut behind him.

"And just what, exactly, do you know about my employer?"

Victoria looked past him, to the closed doors. "Please. Let me out of..."

He reached out and clasped her shoulders. His hands were hard on her flesh.

"Just—just what everyone knows. That—that he likes his privacy."

His jaw thrust forward. "He prefers it, yes. That doesn't make it paranoid."

"Please. I don't—I can't..." Her voice faded. The air seemed to be draining from the elevator. And he was standing so close to her; she could smell the scent of his musky cologne, see the dangerous glitter in the depths of his eyes. Craig had been this close to her, he had been filled with anger, he had——

Don't hurt me, she thought, and then the elevator walls began to shimmer.

"Lady! Hey! Come on, don't pass out on me. Hey! Damn it to hell!"

She heard the muttered curse, and then she was being drawn forward into his arms.

I'm all right, she wanted to say. But the effort seemed too great. She was having a hard enough time not falling into the gray whirlpool that was trying to suck her under, she was . . .

When she came to, she was in the lobby, sitting in a chair. There was a damp cloth on her forehead, and the security man was kneeling beside her, his eyes locked on her face.

"Are you okay?"

Victoria nodded. "Yes." She cleared her throat. "Yes, I'm fine."

He stared at her, and then he puffed out his breath. "I'm sorry," he said, and she knew from the way he'd said it that apologies were foreign to him. "I didn't mean to frighten you."

She smiled a little as she took the cloth from her brow. "You didn't."

A muscle twitched in his jaw. "Yeah, I did. You kept asking me not to hurt you."

A flush rose in her cheeks. "Did I?" He nodded, and she shrugged her shoulders. "Well, you're—you're very intimidating."

He looked at her for another few seconds, and then he rose to his feet.

"Listen." His voice was flat. "This is San Juan, not the Midwest."

Victoria stared at him. "How did you know I . . . ?"

He smiled, this time without malice, and the smile transformed him. The harshness in his face fled, and for the first time Victoria realized how very good-looking he really was.

"You sound like somewhere around the Great Lakes," he said. "Wisconsin, maybe?"

She let out her breath. "Oh. My accent."

He laughed softly. "Your accent."

Victoria rose to her feet. He reached out and touched her shoulder lightly.

"Look, let me call a taxi."

"No." She shook her head again. "Thank you, but I—I feel like walking. I just need to get some air."

His hand slipped away from her. She turned toward the door and started toward it. Each step felt like a dozen. What a mess she'd made of things! First the guard, and now this plainclothes security man—they would never forget her face. Slipping past them again to find Campbell's office would be impossible. She'd have to stand in the street, hide behind the trees that lined the avenue, watch for Campbell and watch for these two at the same time.

"Hey."

She was almost at the door when his voice, low-pitched but hard as steel, stopped her. She drew in her breath and turned and faced him.

"Remember what I told you," he said. "This is the Caribbean, not the States. Things happen here."

"I don't understand."

"There are all kinds of crazies in these islands."

She frowned. "What has that to do with me?"

"American corporations have been targets in the past. People—innocent-looking people—walk in off the streets and do some weird things."

She was stunned. "Is that what you thought? That I was——"

He shrugged. "Anything is possible."

A new fear clutched at her. "Is that why your boss— Mr. Campbell—is that why he's so secretive? Is he—is his chi...his family in danger?"

"No, of course not. I'm just trying to make you see why——" He fell silent, and his eyes turned cold again. "Why all this interest in Campbell, anyway?"

Her heart skipped a beat. "I just—it's not right that anyone live in fear, that's all."

He looked at her for a long moment, and then his lips drew back from his teeth in a tight smile.

"We all fear something. Anyone who doesn't is a damned fool."

He turned, strode to the elevator, and jabbed the control button. There was tension in his shoulders; for some indefinable reason, it made her throat tighten.

Suddenly, he swung toward her. Their eyes met, held, and for an instant that same dizzying whirlpool opened before her. Victoria spun on her heel and stepped quickly toward the electronic doors that led to the street. They slid open and, without a backward glance, she moved out into the sunlight.

CHAPTER TWO

EARLY the next morning, Victoria rented a car and drove into the Hato Rey district. It had been foolish not to have done that right away, but then, everything she'd done yesterday had been foolish. She'd gone waltzing into the Campbell building as if she'd been playing junior detective.

And she'd got off easy. The man who'd accosted her—the chief of security or whatever he was—was not anyone she wanted to confront a second time. Last night, as she'd undressed for bed, she'd paused in front of the mirror, half expecting to find the imprints of his fingers on her shoulders. But the skin had not been bruised; still, in her imagination the steely pressure of his hands was all too real.

A little shudder ran through her as she approached the Campbell building. Whatever happened, she didn't want to run into him again. It had been a minor miracle that he'd let her go—not that there'd been grounds on which to detain her. But he looked like a man who wouldn't give a damn about laws and regulations, a man who lived by a code that was harsh and unforgiving.

There was a little park almost directly opposite the Campbell building. Victoria pulled the car over to the curb, shut off the engine, and settled back in her seat. She had a positive feeling about today. She just knew, in her heart, that things were going to go well. She refused to think about the rest of it, that things *had* to go her way today. She'd only just learned, at breakfast, that the day after tomorrow was a holiday. All the island's businesses would be closed until Monday—which was also the day that she was due to fly back to the States.

The morning passed slowly. At a little past noon, workers streamed from the Campbell building in little groups of two and three. There were some men, but none that resembled the grainy photo in Victoria's purse. She didn't see the security officer, either, which meant that he didn't see her, and that suited her just fine.

Some of the women clutched brown paper sacks. They drifted into the park and settled onto the benches, where they sat chattering in a mixture of Spanish and English while they ate their lunches. Victoria had stopped at a market for some fruit and crackers, but the thought of eating it in the warm, cramped confines of the car wasn't very appealing.

She took a floppy brimmed sun hat from the back seat, twisted her dark hair into a quick topknot, then jammed the hat on her head. A quick glance in the mirror was reassuring. Between the drooping brim and her over-size sunglasses, her face was barely recognizable.

The women didn't even give her a glance as she strolled toward them. She chose a bench that gave her a view of the street through a flowering shrub, ate her meager lunch, then pulled a guidebook from her shoulder bag and settled in for the long afternoon.

The hours dragged, and the warm, flower-scented air made Victoria drowsy. After a while, she closed the book and made a game of people watching. The tourists were easy to spot. The women, and the men, too, were dressed much as she was, in casual cotton shirts and light pants. Most of them looked as if sitting under a shady tree was the best thing that had happened to them all day. There were leathery-looking old men who sat with their faces turned up to the sun, just as they did in the courthouse square back home.

Victoria tried not to think how conspicuous she must seem, sitting here hour after hour. If she had to return tomorrow, she'd have to come up with a better plan—but she tried not to think about that. The day wasn't over yet.

At a few minutes past six, workers began streaming from the Campbell building. Victoria waited until the last straggler had hurried up the street, and then she got to her feet, disappointment lying heavy as stone in her breast. So much for the fruits of her surveillance, she thought, as she trudged disconsolately toward the park exit—and then, suddenly, a sleek black car swept around the corner and pulled up in front of the building.

Victoria's breath caught. She hung back, telling herself it might mean nothing.

A uniformed chauffeur stepped from the car. The electronic doors of the building whooshed open, and a man hurried out. He wore wire-rimmed spectacles, he had a receding hairline——

"Yes," Victoria said. "Oh, yes!"

A woman pushing a baby carriage looked at her strangely. Victoria smiled.

"It's him," she said. "It's——" The woman smiled a little nervously, and Victoria shook her head and laughed. "I'm sorry—*perdón*—I just..."

Was she crazy? Here she stood, babbling like an idiot, and Campbell was already climbing into the back seat of the car. Quickly, she dug her keys from the depths of her shoulder bag and flew toward her rental car.

"Come on," she whispered as she slipped behind the wheel, "damn it, come on!"

The black car was already pulling into traffic. Victoria took a quick glance at the mirror, then jammed her foot on the pedal and swung into a U-turn that sent her car squealing across the centre of the road. Her tires bounced over the curb, then hit the blacktop, and she stepped on the accelerator again.

She'd found the man she'd come thousands of miles to see, and she wasn't going to lose him now.

Staying behind the car wasn't easy. Traffic was heavy, the streets choked with vehicles and people. Cars edged in and out of their lanes, horns blared, lights blinked all too swiftly from green to red. Somehow, however, she managed to keep the vehicle in sight, even though it meant ignoring the angry curses of other drivers and twice sailing through intersections after the light had changed.

Eventually, they merged onto a wide highway that led south, away from the city. The black car picked up speed and Victoria did, too, although she was careful to stay back. There was no point in pushing her luck.

She followed as the car veered off at an exit ramp. A right-hand turn, then a left, and suddenly water glinted ahead. A sign appeared. *Club Náutico*, it said.

Even Victoria's high-school Spanish was enough for that translation. They were heading toward a yacht club.

A handsome white and pink stucco structure, probably a leftover from the island's colonial past, came up quickly. But the black car swept past it, stopping at last when it reached the docks where sleek-hulled pleasure craft bobbed gently on the blue green water.

Victoria braked the rental car. The man she'd been trailing stepped out into the sunlight and began walking briskly along the pier. The limousine driver made a U-turn, and the big car rolled toward her. She averted her face as it approached, but it never hesitated. She glanced into her mirror, watching as it rounded the curve then vanished from sight.

With a sinking heart, she saw L.R. Campbell walk briskly toward a cabin cruiser that lay at the end of the pier. He clambered aboard, waved to a bare-chested man lolling in the cockpit of a motorboat moored nearby, and then Victoria heard the low thrum of an engine. She watched helplessly as Campbell's boat edged from the dock and began making its way out to sea.

Now what? Had she come all this distance only to run into another dead end? Campbell might return in an hour; he might return tomorrow. For all she knew, he might be heading off for a long weekend on the water.

It would be dark soon. Would it be safe to pull off into the parking area and wait? Or——

The cough of an engine starting carried toward her on the warm air. The man in the motorboat was leaning over the side, reaching for his mooring lines. He had greeted Campbell. Maybe he would know where Campbell was heading and how long he'd be gone.

The last line came free. "Wait!" Victoria yelled. She wrenched open the door of the car and raced toward the water. "Wait!" she called again, waving her arms crazily. "Please—*señor*."

The man turned and looked at her. *"Sí?"*

"Por favor," she said breathlessly, *"la barca—donde esta la—la barca—"* So much for high-school Spanish. Victoria muttered a short, unladylike word under her breath. "Do you speak English?"

The man smiled. *"Sí."*

"Please—do you know where the boat's going?"

He shrugged. "I have no idea."

A hollow feeling spread within her. "Well then—do you know when it'll return?"

"I am sorry, I do not."

"But you must know. You must have some idea——"

He looked at her. "I cannot help you, *señorita*."

After a moment, Victoria nodded. *"Gracias,"* she said softly. She watched as he pushed the throttles forward. Within seconds, his boat was pulling out into the harbor.

She stood staring blindly out to sea, and then she turned and walked slowly to where her car stood abandoned in the narrow roadway, the driver's door standing open like a bird with a broken wing. By the time she reached it, there was a tight lump lodged in her throat. She sank back against the side and took a deep, shuddering breath.

What next? She had botched everything. The private detective had been right; she was incapable of handling this on her own. She'd spent almost all her money, she'd come thousands of miles, and for what? To waste time, that was all; time that was precious, time that was——

A horn blared harshly. Victoria spun around. A car had come around the curve and was barreling down the narrow road toward her. It skidded dangerously on the gravel as its driver stood hard on the brakes and the horn blared again. But it was too late. She watched in horror as the car slammed into the open door of her car. The door rose into the air like a missile, turning over and over before coming to rest yards away, the jarring impact of the crash reverberating through her, and then, as if in slow motion, she was on the ground, fighting to draw air into her lungs.

A car door slammed, a man bent over her. Victoria tried to focus her eyes on his face. He was asking her a question, over and over, and after a few seconds, the words began to sort themselves out and make sense.

"Are you all right?" he was saying.

Was she? She swallowed carefully, moved her arms, then her legs. There was a dull throb in her temple, where she'd hit it as she fell, and all her bones felt as if an army had marched over them. But everything seemed to work.

"I—I think so," she said carefully. She put out her hand and pressed her palm flat against the ground. "Let me just see if I can——"

"Don't move." It was a command, not a suggestion. "First let's see what damage you've done."

She fell back and let him move his hands lightly over her. She still couldn't see his face—he was a dark blur silhouetted against the sun that was beginning its plunge to the horizon. But his touch was impersonal and efficient. When he had finished, he leaned back on his heels.

"Well, you seem to be in one piece. You're going to have one hell of a lump here, though."

She hissed and pulled back from his hand when he touched her temple. The sudden motion made her stomach feel as if it were turning over.

"Does that hurt?"

"Of course it hurts." Victoria raised her hand to her face and touched the bruised spot gingerly. It was already swollen, and she could feel a faint trickle of something warm and wet on her fingertips. "Am I bleeding?"

"Yes. It's just a little cut." She felt the soft press of cloth against her skin. "Here, hold this against it for a couple of minutes."

It was his handkerchief. The faint scent of a musky cologne rose to her nostrils, bringing with it a sudden disorientation.

"Are you sure you're okay?"

"Yes," she said quickly. "I'm fine. I just—I'll feel better once I'm on my feet."

He clasped her shoulders as she began to rise. "I don't think you ought to get up just yet," he said. "Why don't you stay put while I get——?"

"No. I don't need any help." Her voice was sharp. There was something about the way he held her that seemed familiar. If she could just concentrate on that. "I—I want to sit up. I know I'll feel better when I do."

She sensed his reluctance as he helped ease her up against the car. "How's that?"

"Better." If only she could see his face... She smiled shakily and held out his handkerchief. "I've probably ruined this."

He laughed. The sound of it was vaguely unpleasant. "Don't worry about it. If it makes you feel any better, I'll have my insurance company tack it on to your bill."

"My bill?"

"They should get a laugh out of it, anyway. Repairs to my 'vette, ten thousand dollars. One linen handkerchief, five bucks additional."

Victoria's mouth dropped open. "You've got to be joking."

"Just take a look at what you did to the front of my car."

"You hit *me*," she said, "I didn't hit——"

"I hit your *car*, lady. Not you, although it's a miracle I *didn't* hit you. What the hell was your car doing, standing in the middle of the damned road?"

"That won't change the facts. You were speeding, and you ran into my car."

"The *facts*, lady, are that your car was in the middle of the road. Look, this is getting us nowhere. Let's let the courts decide who was wrong, okay?" He slipped his arm around her shoulders. "Do you want to try standing now?"

Victoria drew back. "Not with your help," she said coldly.

"Wait a minute. You can't just——"

She rose quickly, pulling away from him as she did. The sun seemed to grow suddenly brighter, and then the earth tilted beneath her feet and she swayed. The stranger caught her to him, his arm curving tightly around her, and he half carried her to his car.

"Here," he said, wrenching open the door, "sit down."

"I—I'm fine."

"Is that why you almost passed out?"

"I didn't almost..." Her voice faded, and a little chill went through her. There it was again, that sense that there was something familiar about him, that——— "Hey!" Her voice rose in shaky indignation as he pulled the floppy-brimmed sun-hat from her head. "What are you doing?"

"I want to check your scalp for bruises. I should have done it before. Bend forward."

"I told you, I'm fine. All I need is an adhesive bandage for the cut on my forehead."

"Bend forward," he repeated. His fingers pressed lightly against her head, and she had no choice but to tilt her head toward him.

"Nothing there. Look up and let me see your eyes."

"My—my eyes?" Victoria's voice faltered. His voice was familiar. She knew him. She——

"Yes. I want to check for concussion."

"I don't have a concussion. Really. I—I——"

Oh, God.

It all came together at once. Of course she knew him. The man who'd run into her car was the same man who'd made her life such hell yesterday at Campbell Enterprises.

And, if she had figured it out, then it was only a matter of minutes until he did, too. Until now, he'd been caught up in the aftermath of the accident. Her sun hat had put him off, too, and her oversize dark glasses...

"Raise your head, please."

Instead, Victoria leaned further forward. Her hair fell around her cheeks.

"Look, I appreciate your concern. But I'm fine. Really. And—and I'm in a bit of a rush. So——"

"Yes. I'll just bet you are."

Was it her imagination, or was there a sudden dangerous edge in his voice? She fought against the awful desire to look up and see the expression on his face. It was like driving past the scene of an accident; you didn't want to look, but there was always that morbid sense of curiosity that urged you to turn your head, no matter what the risk.

She took another deep breath. "Why don't you just give me the name of your insurance company? My car's a rental, and I took full coverage. I'll tell the company the accident was my fault entirely. I'm sure there'll be no——" her voice faltered as he stepped closer to her "—no problem."

"Take off your glasses." His tone was silken and dangerous, and she knew the second she heard it that the game was up.

Victoria shook her head. "No."

"Take them off."

She shrank back. "No. I mean, what for? I told you, I'm perfectly..."

She made a little sound as he reached down and whipped the glasses from her nose. There was a long silence, and then he let out his breath.

"Well, well, well," he said softly. "Isn't it a small world?"

She looked up slowly into eyes as flat and colorless as winter ice. Suddenly, she was very aware of how alone they were.

"It's—it's not how it looks," she said quickly.

He rocked back on his heels and gave her a smile that matched the coldness in his eyes.

"Isn't it?"

"No. I—I..." Think. *Think!* There had to be something she could say, some explanation she could offer.

She recoiled as he leaned forward and slammed his hands on the doorframe on either side of her.

"Well? Why were you following me?"

Victoria blinked. "Following you?"

"Come on, don't try playing the innocent. It worked once, but——"

"Is that what you think? That I was following *you*?" Despite herself, she laughed. "Why on earth would I do that?"

For the first time, a look of uncertainty glinted in his eyes. "You tell me."

"And *how* could I have followed you?" she said, ignoring his question. "I was here first, remember?"

He stared at her while the seconds ticked away, and finally he nodded. "So you were."

Her pulse began to ease. "Well, then——"

"Let me get this straight. You just happened to wander into the Campbell building yesterday."

"I told you, I was looking for a job."

"And now, by the strangest coincidence you found your way here, to my yacht club."

"*Your* yacht club?" It took no effort at all to achieve a tone of disbelief. "I didn't know that."

He smiled tightly. "Didn't you?"

"Look, I was out driving, seeing the island—and—and I saw a sign that said something about boats..."

"There are a dozen places to rent boats along this stretch of road."

"Well, I didn't know that. I was just—I was out driving, and I—I saw the sign. I knew it said something about boats, and I thought—I thought I'd see about—about renting one."

She fell silent and waited for him to say something. But he didn't; he just kept looking at her, his expression absolutely unreadable. After a moment, she swallowed dryly and began to step out of his car.

"Where are you going?" His voice was very soft. Something about it sent a tremor along her spine.

"I—I'm feeling much steadier." She looked up at him and smiled. Her lips felt as if they were being stretched across her face. "I'm just going to get the insurance papers from my car and——"

"That won't be necessary."

"Well, thank you for that. But you're right, this was my fault entirely."

His teeth drew back from his lips in a cool smile. "Yes, it certainly was. Now, if you'll come with me, please?"

Victoria stared at him. "What?"

"Neither of these cars will be going anywhere, not without a tow truck."

She looked from his car to hers. He was right, of course. She didn't have to be a mechanic to know that neither automobile would be heading back to San Juan on its own.

"Now what?" she asked wearily.

The stranger slammed the door, then went around to the driver's side, pausing only long enough to run a hand over the Corvette's mangled front. Then he reached inside and removed the keys from the ignition.

"What's your name?" he said.

She hesitated. She couldn't tell him her name. If he ever mentioned her to his employer, it might ring a bell in the mind of the ever-suspicious L.R. Campbell. Her name was on her baby's birth certificate, after all, and Campbell might think she'd come here to make trouble. And she hadn't; the last thing she wanted was to upset her child's life. She only wanted——

"Well?" She looked up. The man was watching her narrowly. "Did that lump on your head give you amnesia?"

"Victoria," she said, "Victoria Hamilton."

"Well, Miss Hamilton, what we'll do now is arrange for that tow. And we'll see if we can't get that cut of yours cleaned and bandaged."

Her face lit up. Maybe she would salvage something from this day, after all. She could do more than phone for a tow at the clubhouse; she could ask some discreet questions about L.R. Campbell, perhaps even arrange for a boat rental for tomorrow morning.

She frowned as he took her arm and began walking her toward the water. "The clubhouse is the other way, isn't it?" The man beside her didn't answer. "Excuse me. Isn't the clubhouse behind us?"

He glanced at her, then back toward the docks. "Yes."

A pulse began to beat in her temple, just above where she'd cut it. "Why aren't we going there, then?"

"It's after eight. The clubhouse is closed for the night."

"Well, then, take me to a telephone. There must be one near by."

Water glinted ahead, its surface afire with the crimson and orange of the setting sun, silhouetting a sleek cruiser that rolled lazily on the swell. The man beside her paused, one hand on her arm, the other fishing in his pocket for a key ring.

Victoria stumbled against him, fighting the sudden panic rising inside her.

"What are you doing?"

"Let's go, Miss Hamilton".

"No. You said you were taking me to a phone." She cried out as he lifted her into his arms. "Put me down. Do you hear me?" She hammered wildly at his shoulders as he shifted her weight and began striding briskly along the slip toward the boat. "What in God's name do you think you're doing?"

"You need a phone and a first-aid kit," he said calmly. "And I'm taking you where you can find both."

"To that boat, you mean?" Victoria pounded his shoulders harder. "Are you crazy? I'm not going to set foot on that thing. And I'm going to report you to your employer. You can count on it, Mr.—Mr.——"

He looked down at her as she struggled in his arms, and a smile curved across his mouth.

"That's right, we haven't introduced ourselves properly, have we?" His next words almost made her heart stop beating. "I'm L.R. Campbell, Miss Hamilton." He laughed softly. "But, considering how well we've come to know each other in the past couple of days, I don't think even Emily Post would object if you called me Roarke."

CHAPTER THREE

IMPOSSIBLE! This man wasn't the one she'd been searching for. L.R. Campbell was older. He was—he was sedate, even staid. He was the sort of man who'd be comfortable beside a fireplace on a cool evening, who'd be content having a sleepy child cuddle in his lap.

Nothing of that description fitted the man holding her in his arms. He emanated power and vitality, not comfort. He would know nothing about children—but everything about women. The way he held her, the way he'd looked at her, even when he was angry, told her that.

He *couldn't* be L.R. Campbell. He had to be an impostor; but that didn't matter right now because whoever he was, he was striding off with her, carrying her on board the boat that he claimed was his. Victoria's heart thudded with fear.

"Put me down!" She pounded against his shoulders again, hard enough so that she felt the energy of the blows reverberate through her wrists and up her arms, but he didn't pause or miss a step. "Damn you—put me down, or I'll scream."

"Scream all you like. The gulls will be happy to join in."

"I don't know what you think you're doing, but you won't get away with it. Do you hear me? I swear, I'll——"

"You've read too many bad novels, Miss Hamilton." A slow smile tilted across his mouth as he set her down in the cockpit. "Or indulged in too many fantasies. The white slave trade's been dead in these islands for years."

Victoria faced him angrily, chin elevated and eyes glittering. "Look, Mr.—Mr. Whoever-You-Are..."

"I told you my name."

"Yes," she said grimly. "You'd like me to believe you're L.R. Campbell."

The brilliance of the tropical sunset had given way to velvety night, and his face, with its look of amused derision, was clearly visible in the bright glow of the stars.

"Roarke. How much better acquainted must we be before you call me that?"

He was laughing at her, damn him. And he sounded so convincing. A chill danced along her skin. Could he— was it conceivable that he really was...?

A sharp pain flared in her temple. No. He wasn't. She couldn't let herself think that way; not if everything she'd believed for the last two years was to have any meaning.

"You're not L.R. Campbell," she said coldly.

The glint left his eyes. All at once, his face turned hard and menacing.

"And you weren't here by accident."

"I told you how that happened. I—I saw the sign, and——"

"I've already heard the story, Miss Hamilton. I'm supposed to believe you've turned up like a bad penny, two days running, purely by accident."

Her flush deepened. "It—it's the truth."

"Because you say so?"

"I'm not in the habit of telling lies," she said stiffly.

He smiled coolly. "Fascinating. Neither am I."

Victoria stared at him. If he'd planned on attacking her, he was certainly going about it strangely. The pain flared in her temple, sharper this time. Suddenly, she knew that he'd only brought her here for the reasons he'd claimed—which might mean that everything else he'd told her was true.

The boat rolled gently on the swell, and her stomach rolled along with it.

"Are you all right?"

No. She was not all right. Things were coming apart right in front of her. And the pain in her head was—was——

"Miss Hamilton." His hands cupped her shoulders. "Are you okay"

"Yes," she said. She dredged up a bright smile and looked at him. "Just—just a little tired. It's been a long day."

His mouth narrowed as he let go of her. "One that hasn't ended yet," he said, selecting one of the keys from the ring in his hand. He unlocked the cabin door and reached inside. Lights blazed on, illuminating the deck and what was visible of the area below. "Let's get started, shall we? I'll tend to that cut, and then I'll phone for a tow truck."

"And a taxi."

"And a taxi," he said, as he made his way down the steps. Victoria hesitated for a long moment, and then she drew a deep breath into her lungs and carefully followed after him.

The main cabin was much larger than she'd expected—larger than her living room back home, and certainly more handsomely furnished.

"Sit down wherever you like," he said, his hand sweeping out in an imperious gesture that took up the entire area. She hesitated, then perched gingerly on the edge of a mahogany table, watching as he stripped off his jacket and tie, then unbuttoned his cuffs and rolled his shirtsleeves to his elbows. He slid back a wall panel, revealing neatly stacked shelves on which sat gauze pads, bottles of antiseptic, and assorted tins and bottles of tablets. "Right," he said. "Now, just tilt your head up to the light."

But Victoria wasn't listening. She was staring, instead, at a framed photograph on the bulkhead wall next to him. It was a shot of a man standing beside an enormous billed fish.

ROARKE CAMPBELL TAKES RECORD MARLIN, the headline read, and all the slim hopes she'd clung to during the past half hour fell away. The man in the photo and the man standing in front of her, waiting impatiently for her to lift her head for his ministrations, were one and the same.

"I'm not going to do surgery, if that's what's worrying you."

She looked at him. He was laughing—at her, she knew—and why wouldn't he? She probably looked as if she was about to faint. It took all the strength she possessed to offer him a smile in return.

"It—it's the antiseptic," she said, nodding toward the open bottle he'd placed on the table beside her. "The smell of it takes me back to when I was little. I fell and cut my knee, and—and I had to have it stitched."

"This cut's too small for stitches," he said, frowning as he drew her hair back from her temple. "Tell me if it hurts."

It might have hurt; she had no way of knowing. Her head was whirling as she tried to sort out everything that was happening. Had Dr. Ronald lied to her?

"Are you sure my baby's going to a good home?" she'd said anxiously that last morning, and he'd put his arm around her shoulders and assured her that he'd personally chosen the people who were adopting her child.

"Good, solid folks," he'd said, "the both of them."

Her eyes flickered across Campbell's face. He was swabbing the cut, his mouth narrowed in concentration. Would she—would anyone—call him good and solid?

No. There were better ways to describe that hard, almost harsh face with its square jaw and piercing eyes with their dark, thick lashes.

". . . looked at. All right?"

Victoria blinked. She looked up, and their eyes met. "I—I'm sorry," she said quickly. "Did you—did you say something?"

"I said, what really matters is this bump on your head, not the cut. Does it hurt when I touch it?"

His fingers brushed lightly across her skin. His touch was cool, soothing against her flesh. She swallowed, then pulled back.

"A little."

He frowned. "You might want to have a doctor take a look when you get to San Juan."

"I—I don't think the cut will scar."

"Neither do I." His gaze swept over her face, lingering for a heartbeat on her parted lips. "It would be a pity to let anything spoil such a——" His frown deepened, and suddenly he stepped away from her. "Well," he said briskly, "that's taken care of. Now for the phone calls. If you give me the name of the rental agency, I'll notify them for you, while I'm at it."

Victoria nodded. He was taking charge of things easily, as if he did this every day of his life. Well, that was dumb. He *did* do this every day of his life. He was the head of a company that bore his name. He was L.R. Campbell.

Her head felt as if someone were trying to punch a hole through it. She turned away quickly and made her way carefully up the steps into the open cockpit. The air had cooled a little, just enough so that the wind coming in from the open sea sent a feathery chill along her flesh. She pushed the hair back from her eyes, leaned her arms on the railing, and stared out over the water.

It was peaceful here, with no sound except the sigh of the wind and the creak of the mooring lines, but she'd have traded all that tranquillity for the security of her San Juan hotel room. There was so much to sift through, so much to try to sort out, and she couldn't do it here, not with Roarke in the cabin. Just seeing him was confusing enough; to try to imagine him as her child's adoptive father was impossible.

Unless—unless he wasn't. Victoria's heart lifted a little. Campbell was really a fairly common name. Maybe the detective had found the wrong man. Yes. That had to be it. Yes. To think anything else was insane. Dr. Ronald wouldn't have deceived her. He'd guided her through the darkest days of her life, and he'd never once let her down, not even on that terrible last morning, when she'd almost lost her courage.

He'd stepped into her hospital room and found her huddled in bed, sobbing her heart out into the pillow.

"Victoria," he'd said, in that soothing voice she'd come to rely on, "what is it, dear? Come, you can tell me."

Victoria had shaken her head. "I can't—I don't—giving my baby away——" she'd whispered. "I don't think I can go through with it."

"Look at me, dear." Slowly, she'd raised her tear-stained face to the doctor's. "You can't keep this child. You know how ill your mother is, and you know the news that you've borne a baby out of wedlock might well finish her."

The words were harsh, but there was no denying their truth. Bess Winters had suffered her third heart attack in two years just a little more than five months before. It had been the deciding factor in the terrible decision Victoria had made, although not the only one. Even if her mother had been well, what could she have offered her child except a sad replay of her own unhappy life?

"I know," she'd said finally, through her tears. "But— but giving her up without seeing her, without counting her fingers and toes..."

The doctor had taken her hands in his. "Trust me, Victoria. You baby is healthy and perfect."

Victoria had looked up at him pleadingly. "Does she— does she look like me?"

His face had softened a little. "I suppose she does." Victoria's eyes had filled, and the doctor had cleared his throat. "Seeing her will only make it harder for you. Trust me, dear. The people who are adopting her will love her very much."

"You've met them?"

The doctor's eyes had slipped away from hers. "Of course. That's the good thing about private adoptions, Victoria. One can make the best choice possible."

Victoria drew a shuddering breath as the night wind ruffled the waters of the Caribbean. Yes. That was what he'd said, and it had made sense. He'd known her all her life, he'd known exactly the kind of parents she'd want for her child: a mother and father who'd love her child as much as they loved each other. She'd even formed a mental picture of them, which was why she'd felt as if she were almost seeing a familiar face when the private investigator had produced the photo of the man he'd misidentified as Campbell.

To have all that disintegrate in an instant was staggering. It was almost more than she could comprehend. It was...

"Bad news."

She spun toward the cabin. The sudden movement sent a bolt of pain rocketing through her skull.

"What is?" she said, touching her hand lightly to her head.

Roarke's face was twisted into a dark scowl. He stepped on deck and leaned back against the opposite railing.

"No taxi."

Victoria's brows arched. "What do you mean, no taxi?"

"Did I say that in an incomprehensible tongue, Miss Hamilton?" His voice was cold. "I phoned three companies, but the answer was the same each time. Nothing—except for the last place. They said they'd send a car in a couple of hours."

"But it's barely eight."

"Precisely."

She drew herself up. His attitude had changed again. He was as hostile as he'd been when the accident had first occurred, and she was damned if she knew why.

"I don't know why you sound so irritated," she said sharply. "I'm the one who'll have to cool my heels for the next two hours, not you."

Roarke's jaw thrust forward. "If you hadn't left your car in the middle of the road in the first place——"

"Oh, please. Let's not go into that tired old routine again."

He glowered at her, and then he puffed out his breath. "You're right," he said, although the look on his face clearly told her he didn't mean that at all. "What's done is done. We need to deal with the present, don't we?"

The breeze tossed Victoria's hair across her face, and she pushed her hand into it and thrust it back behind her ear.

"What about a car rental agency? Perhaps they'd agree to deliver a car here." Roarke laughed sharply, and her chin lifted. "Did I say something amusing?"

"This is Puerto Rico, Miss Hamilton, not Chicago. No one's interested in working at this hour."

"You could try."

"I already have."

Silence settled between them, and then Victoria sighed. "Well, then, I guess I'll just have to sit in my car and wait until——"

"Not until. *If*. The taxi company said they'd send a car; but I wouldn't want to stake my life on it."

She stared out at the docks. There were street lamps strung along its perimeter but not all the bulbs had come on, and the ones that had cast only faint, yellow beams of light. The parking area and the road where her disabled car lay abandoned were swathed in darkness.

A little shudder went through her. "The road's not all that far," she said with a great deal more enthusiasm than she felt. "A mile, perhaps."

"It's at least four miles to the highway. Surely not even you would be foolish enough to attempt that by yourself."

"Look, Mr.——" His brows rose, and she swallowed. "Roarke," she said. Actually, it was easier to call him that than to call him by the name of the man who'd sailed off on a cabin cruiser almost two hours ago. "As you said, it's the present we have to deal with."

He glared at her, and then he nodded his head reluctantly. "You're right."

"So if you've any suggestions...?"

"Only one." He seemed to draw himself up before he spoke, and Victoria sensed that whatever he was about to say was distasteful to him. "You can come with me."

She gaped at him. "On your boat?"

"Yes."

"You mean, you'd take me back to San Juan? Oh, but I couldn't let you do that. It's——"

"Don't be ridiculous. That would take hours." He turned away, leaned across the railing, and began hauling in a mooring line. "I'll take you to Isla de la Pantera.

From there, I can make arrangements to have you taken back to San Juan.''

"What is Isla de—de . . . ?"

". . . de la Pantera." He hesitated. "It's where I live."

Victoria's eyes widened. She had spent the past two days doing everything but getting herself run over to learn his address, and now . . .

"Well?" He put his hands on his hips and looked at her. "Make up your mind, please, Miss Hamilton. Are you going with me or are you staying here?"

"How could I turn down such a hospitable invitation?" she said sweetly.

His eyes narrowed. "I take it that's a 'yes.' "

She smiled. "You take it right," she said, and she sank down into the cockpit seat and looked placidly out to sea.

Victoria swallowed carefully. Her stomach felt as if it were somewhere in her throat, but at least she'd been able to stop herself from being sick all over the teak cockpit. She cast a quick look at Roarke Campbell, standing with his back to her at the wheel. Somehow, she doubted if he'd much appreciate her losing her lunch all over his highly polished deck.

Not that she'd had lunch, just the fruit and crackers hours ago in that little park. Still, her stomach was queasy. Worse than queasy. It rose and fell with each swell of the waves.

And her head. She lifted her hand and touched the bump on it lightly. The pain was steady now, beating in tempo with her heart.

She sighed and put her head back. All in all, she felt absolutely rotten.

Not that Roarke had noticed. The trip to the island would take just half an hour, he'd said, but it felt as if they'd been slamming through the sea for twice that now, and in all that time he hadn't once looked at her or spoken a word.

She knew why, of course. This man who guarded his private life so zealously, whose address had been harder to find than a winning lottery number, was taking her to his very doorstep with him.

Well, not his doorstep. He would put her in a taxi and deposit her at an inn or a café while he arranged for her transportation back to the mainland. But she wasn't going back, not tonight anyway. She would thank him for all his help, then tell him the accident had left her feeling rocky—which wasn't any exaggeration at all—and that she'd decided to stay the night on Isla de la Pantera. Then, in the morning, she'd scout out the Campbell house and take a quick look at it, just to confirm what she already knew, that she'd been sent on a wild-goose chase. This was L.R. Campbell, all right—but not the L.R. Campbell who'd adopted her baby. Wait until she got home again. That damned private investigator had wasted her time and money, but most of all he'd given her false hope. Now she'd have to start all over again.

The engine's growling roar fell to a whisper. Victoria looked up as the boat slowed. She started to rise to her feet but the deck seemed to tilt out from beneath her. She slid back into her seat, blinking with surprise.

"What was that?" she said.

Roarke turned toward her. "What was what?"

Victoria looked up at him. "Why did the boat——" Why were there two of him instead of one? "I— I——" She swallowed and closed her eyes. "I just— I don't seem to have my sea legs yet."

He looked at her, then he held out his hand. "Well, you're never going to get them sitting there," he said brusquely. "Take my hand and come on over here."

She did, carefully, clutching his hand as if it were a lifeline. Slowly, she stepped up beside him and looked out over the water. Lights glittered in the near distance, and she could make out shapes—boats at anchor, she thought, but it was difficult to be certain. Every outline seemed superimposed on another.

A tremor went through her, and Roarke looked down at her. "What is it?"

"Nothing," she said quickly. She glanced up and saw that two Roarkes were still watching her. "Nothing," she repeated, but there was a shakiness in her voice that even she could hear.

Roarke's scowl deepened. "Are you cold?" He slipped his arm around her before she could answer. His body felt warm and she had to force herself to refrain from burrowing into it for comfort. "You should have said something—there are sweaters below."

"I—I'm not cold. I just——" Her stomach rose again, this time flooding her mouth with bile. She winced as she swallowed. "I don't feel very well, that's all."

He turned her toward him. "What do you mean? Are you seasick?"

She started to shake her head, then thought better of it.

"No. At least, I don't think so."

Roarke put his hand under her chin and tilted her face to his. "You're as white as a sheet."

She drew a breath. "I—I feel strange."

"For God's sake," he said harshly, "can't you be more specific than that?"

Victoria gave him a dazzling smile, but neither of the two Roarkes smiled at her in return.

"Yes," she said, "I can. I can see two of everything."

His arm tightened around her. "Jesus."

"And——" Her smile fled, and she moaned. "And I'm going to be sick."

And, with explosive violence, she was.

*   *   *

Somewhere in the distance a bell was ringing, its tone deep and steady. It was a soothing sound, like the church bells back home.

"Victoria."

"Mmm."

"Toria." A hand brushed lightly over her cheek. "Come on, wake up."

She sighed and tried to burrow into the pillows. "I'm tired," she murmured.

The hand brushed her face again, then moved to her shoulder. "Can you open your eyes and talk to me? Just for a moment, I promise, and then I'll let you go back to sleep."

Slowly, slowly, Victoria forced her eyes open. At first, all she saw was a velvety blackness. Then, little by little, things began to come into focus. Moonlight, streaming through a set of french windows. Sheer lace curtains, moving gently under the touch of the breeze.

And a man's face, inches from hers. A man, bending over her as she lay in the center of a wide, soft bed.

"Roarke?" She started to sit up, and fireworks went off inside her head.

"Easy," Roarke said softly. He cupped her shoulders and gently laid her back on the pillows.

Victoria swallowed. Her mouth and throat were dry as sand. "Where—where am I?" she whispered.

He laughed softly. "I always wondered if people really asked that when they came to."

She blinked. Just for a second, there'd been two of him smiling at her, one mirroring the other like flickering ghost images on an out-of-focus TV screen.

"Come to? What do you mean?"

"You passed out on the boat. Don't you remember?"

"No. I—I——" She closed her eyes as fragments of what had happened began coming back. The lights on shore. The swaying deck. The sudden rush of illness...

"Oh, God," she whispered. "I made a mess of your boat, didn't I?"

He smiled. "You were the perfect passenger. Desperate as you were, you somehow made it to the rail."

"But how did I get here? Is this a hospital?"

"No. It's not a hospital."

No, it couldn't be. Even in the darkness, even with things doubling themselves, what she could see of this room spoke of luxury and wealth. He had taken her to a hotel—the island's finest, probably. Well, one night wouldn't wipe out her finances. At least, she hoped it wouldn't.

"How did I get to this hotel, then?"

"It's not a hotel, either." He reached to the nightstand and took a cool cloth from the basin lying there. "Here," he said, spreading the cloth across her brow. "How does that feel?"

"But if it's not a hotel——"

"This is my home."

She stared at him, speechless. His home? She was tucked into a bed in Roarke Campbell's house? God, it was incredible, one of those horrid little tricks the demons of life liked to play from time to time. Only a few hours ago she'd been skulking around like a spy in a B movie doing everything she could to learn where he lived, and now here she was, under his very roof.

Not that it mattered. This was very definitely the wrong——

"Would you like a sip of water?"

She looked up and smiled gratefully. "Yes, please. That would be lovely."

"Here," he said, slipping his arm under her shoulders and lifting her head from the pillow. "Not too much, now. Mendoza says your stomach's going to be touch and go for a while."

Victoria's brow furrowed. "Mendoza?"

Roarke eased her down to the pillows. "My physician. He examined you, took X-rays—you don't remember that, either?"

She shook her head a little, as much as she dared.
"No. I don't remember anything after the boat. I——"

But she did, suddenly: the gently probing hands of a
man with a soft Spanish accent, the faint whirr of a
machine. Roarke, lifting her into his arms, carrying her
up a wide, curving staircase as if she were weightless,
lowering her gently onto this soft, canopied bed...

Her hands flew to her throat. It was bare, and she
knew, instinctively, that the rest of her was naked, too,
under the soft cotton quilt.

Roarke laughed, as if he'd read her mind. "Relax,
Miss Hamilton. It was Constancia who put you to bed."

"Constancia?"

"My housekeeper." He rose from the bedside. "I
suggest you get some sleep now. If you need anything
during the night, there's a bell on the nightstand."

Victoria closed her eyes wearily. "I've bothered you
enough already."

There was a heavy silence, and then Roarke made a
sound that might have been a laugh.

"Yes," he said. "You have. Good night, Victoria
Hamilton. Sleep well."

Color rushed to her cheeks. She had meant the words
as a polite apology; it would have been nice if he could
have managed an equally polite, if insincere, response,
and she opened her eyes and turned her head on the
pillow, ready to tell him so—just in time to see the door
close after him.

She drew a deep breath, then let it out slowly while
she stared at the ribbon of moonlight that lay draped
across the room like an ivory streamer. What a strange
man Roarke Campbell was. He seemed hostile and un-

yielding, yet he had taken care of her in her illness, even brought her here, to his home.

She sighed again, even more deeply. It was just as well he wasn't the man she'd come seeking. He would never do as a father. It was even difficult to imagine him married. A man like that would never find a woman to please him. He was too private, too harsh, too——

She thought suddenly of how he'd held her close to him on the boat, when she'd felt dizzy, of how he'd carried her to this room. She had sensed the repressed power in his touch, the strength of his hard body. What would it be like to feel that body pressed against hers, to tremble in his arms? What would it be like to cry out for his possession . . . ?

A dark flush rose along her skin. Was this what a concussion did to you? Did it make your imagination run riot? Make you think things you'd never, in a million lifetimes, thought before?

"Señorita?" Victoria turned quickly toward the door. A plump, middle-aged woman smiled tentatively at her. "I did not wish to disturb you. But the *señor* thought you might wish some fruit juice."

Victoria swallowed. "No, thank you anyway. I—I don't want anything just now."

"As you like, *señorita.*" The housekeeper smiled again. "If you need me, there is a bell on——"

"Constancia? That is your name, isn't it?" The woman nodded. Victoria touched her tongue to her lips. "I was just wondering—is Señor Campbell married?"

Constancia's eyes seemed to darken. "No," she said after a moment, "he has no wife. Good night, *señorita.*"

Victoria sighed as the door swung shut. Roarke had no wife, just as she'd figured. If she'd had any last, lingering doubt that he was the man she'd set out to find, it was gone.

What a day it had been. She felt as if she'd spent it wandering through a house of mirrors. Things looked real until you got close, and then they turned out to be nothing but illusion.

Like Roarke. Was he cold and unfeeling? Or was there another side to him after all?

Victoria's lashes fluttered to her cheeks. It didn't really matter, she thought hazily. By this time tomorrow, she'd be back in San Juan, and Roarke Campbell would be nothing but a memory. A memory...

Her sigh drifted into the still, night air, and she tumbled into a long, deep sleep.

CHAPTER FOUR

VICTORIA awoke abruptly, without the usual disorientation that came of awakening in a strange room. Even though she could see nothing, she knew where she was.

What had awakened her? A dream. Yes. Something—something about her baby.

She hissed softly as she rolled onto her side. Her head still hurt a little, but she'd got away lucky. She grimaced as she thought of the injuries she might have sustained. But it hadn't been her fault. She had to find her baby...

Didn't she?

She shifted uneasily beneath the soft cotton quilt. Why hadn't she ever asked herself that question before? Maybe because the answer had always seemed obvious. But it didn't now. If anything, her quest seemed hard to justify. The hours she'd spent spying, the accident that had cost two cars and a concussion—that was quite a price to pay for self-indulgence.

The thought made her recoil in horror.

No. It wasn't self-indulgence. It couldn't be. She had a right to see her baby, hadn't she?

She caught her lower lip between her teeth. But considering how badly she'd bungled everything so far, who knew what might happen? Could it be that she would only bring suffering and confusion to her daughter and to the man and woman who loved her? Could she risk that? Was she really that selfish?

Victoria turned on her back, then flung her arm across her eyes. Suddenly, everything that had driven her during the past months seemed blindly egocentric. It was as if

the blow to her head had driven sanity into it. Herself,
that was all she'd considered, and never mind anybody
else—not even her child.

She had to stop her search. God, it was so simple;
had she known it all along? Tears rose in her eyes. There
was nothing to be sad about, she told herself; her little
girl had a happy life somewhere, she was sure of it.

But the tears flowed anyway, and she buried her face
in the pillow and cried until, finally, there were no tears
left.

And then, for the first time in months, Victoria fell
into a dreamless sleep.

When she awoke again, the room was filled with sunlight. There was a dull throb in her temple, but she felt
rested and she knew it was as much because of the decision she'd reached during the night as anything else.

Carefully, making no sudden moves, she inched her
way upright against the pillows. What she wanted right
now was a shower. She looked at the bell on the nightstand. Ring if you need anything, Roarke had said. But
the en suite bath was just across the room; surely she
could get that far on her own?

She pushed back the covers, swung her legs to the floor
and counted to ten, then rose to her feet.

"So far, so good," she said aloud—and then the room
shimmered, as if the sunlight had suddenly exploded all
around her. She grasped the bedpost and clung to it with
both hands. A chill beading of sweat rose on her
forehead, and she glanced again at the bell. If she rang
it, would Constancia answer? Or would Roarke?
Somehow, the thought of Roarke helping her, of his arms
going around her and supporting her, was unsettling.

Images flashed into her mind. Roarke, his hard face
bent over her as she moaned with pain; Roarke, his hands
supporting her as she leaned over a basin; Roarke,

blotting her damp skin with a soft towel, then helping her into an oversize cotton shirt...

Her breath caught as she looked down at herself. She was wearing a man's shirt. Roarke's shirt. She knew it was his, she could smell his scent on the soft fabric, and all at once the memory came again: she felt his hands brushing lightly across her throat as he buttoned her into the shirt, brushing lightly across her breasts.

"Let's go, Victoria," she said briskly, and with grim determination she began the million-mile journey to the bathroom.

She was trembling with exhaustion when she finally reached it. She clutched the rim of the sink, bowed her head until her bones stopped feeling as if they were made of rubber, then lifted her head and peered into the mirror.

"Oh, my God," she whispered.

Laughter rose in her throat. She looked as if she'd gone into the ring with the world's heavyweight boxing champion. Actually, that was putting it kindly. Her skin was pasty, her dark hair a wild tatter. There was a discolored lump the size of a robin's egg on her temple, and yet that was not the worst of it.

Victoria leaned closer to the mirror. Her eyes were not just black and blue, they were pink and purple and violet. It was enough to put any eyeshadow she'd ever tried to shame.

She laughed aloud as she peeled off the shirt and dropped it on the floor. Making her way back to San Juan would be interesting, to say the least. Her oversize dark glasses were where her sun hat was: in the disabled rental car back at the marina. There'd be no disguise to hide behind. Well, she'd remedy that as soon as possible. There had to be a *farmacia* or a *supermercado* near by where she could purchase new glasses, darker and bigger than her old ones, and then she'd head for the ferry or whatever public transportation it was that took people from Isla de la Pantera to San Juan, and she'd put this disastrous trip behind her.

She set the shower to hot, waited until the steam billowed out like the fog rolling in from Lake Michigan, and then she stepped into the stall and closed the door, groaning with pleasure as the hot water cascaded down her body. Once her muscles had unknotted, she washed and rinsed her hair, then turned her face up to the spray.

"Lovely," she sighed—but the sigh turned into a shriek as the shower door was flung open behind her. Hands clamped on to her elbows and lifted her bodily from beneath the spray.

"Incredibly stupid, you mean. You damned little fool," Roarke said furiously. "What in hell did you think you were doing?"

"Roarke," she sputtered, "Roarke, you—you——"

A voluminous bathrobe fell over her shoulders and down her back. "Get that on."

"Damn you, Roarke. How dare you——?"

"Get into the robe." His voice was grim. "We'll talk about what I 'dare' afterward."

Quickly, Victoria shoved her arms into the sleeves, pulled the lapels of the robe together across her breasts, and knotted the sash. Her blood was pounding in her ears, and she spun around to face him without thinking of anything but how he had almost scared the life out of her.

"How dare you?" she said tightly. "How——"

Her face reflected a moment of surprise. Turning toward him that quickly hadn't been a very good idea, she thought with amazing calm, and then her knees buckled. Roarke cursed and scooped her into his arms before she could sink to the floor. When the room stopped spinning, she found herself staring into his hard face.

"Do you specialize in doing whatever damned thing comes into your head?" he said furiously. "Would it be too much to expect that you would once stop and think before you act?"

"Put me down, please," she said in a shaky little voice.

"Why? So you can get into the shower again?" His face grew even darker. "Perhaps you were planning on going for a walk. Or a run. A game of tennis, maybe——"

"Will you please put me down?"

"Gladly." Victoria could hear the rapid thud of his heart beneath her ear as he stalked into the bedroom. He was angry, she thought incredulously. *He* was angry!

"Just what in God's name were you doing?" he said through his teeth.

Victoria's eyes flashed as she looked up at him. "Do you really need to ask?" she said sweetly. "I mean, you must have had a rather good view."

His jaw jutted forward. "Playing Peeping Tom is not one of my hobbies."

"Then what were you doing in my bathroom?"

He gave her a quick, cold smile as he deposited her on the bed. "It's *my* bathroom. And I much prefer it as it is, without crumpled bodies in the shower stall."

"Don't be ridiculous." Her voice rose, following after him as he retraced his steps to the bathroom. "I was doing just fine until you came along and tried to scare me to death."

Roarke reappeared with a bath towel in his hands. "Did I or did I not tell you to ring if you needed help?"

"I didn't need help. I was only——" Her voice grew muffled as he draped the towel over her soaked hair; she caught the ends and twisted them up into a turban. "I was only showering, for heaven's sake. You make it sound as if I were——"

"It was a damned stupid thing to do."

Victoria felt her cheeks blaze with heat. "Look, I know you took me into your home——"

"Only because I had no alternative."

"Is it impossible for you to be pleasant for more than five minutes at a time?"

"I'm simply being honest." He walked to the french windows and opened them, letting in a warm, sea-laden breeze. "Believe me, if there'd been something else to do, I'd have done it."

Her chin lifted. "If you felt that way, why didn't you take me to a hospital?"

He smiled tightly. "There is no hospital on this island."

"Well, then, you could have taken me to an inn. Or a hotel. Or..."

Roarke put his hands on his hips. "I would have, gladly, if there were such a place."

Victoria frowned. "I don't understand. What kind of island is this, anyway?"

His lips drew back from his teeth. "A private one."

"Well, don't the other homeowners——" She broke off, flustered. "What's so funny? Damn it, Roarke, what are you laughing at?"

"Isla de la Pantera is mine," he said softly.

She stared at him. "Yours? You mean, you own it?"

"Exactly." He laughed at the look on her face. "All of it, from the harbor we docked at to the ridge and down to the sea on the other side."

"I see." She drew a breath. "Well, then," she said grudgingly, "I have to be grateful to you for taking me in last night. But——"

"You came here two nights ago, Victoria."

Her mouth dropped open. "What are you talking about?"

Roarke rocked back on his heels and folded his arms across his chest. "Don't you remember?"

"No," she said in a thin voice, "I don't. Are you telling me I—I've been asleep for—for——"

"Unconscious, asleep, call it what you will. You've been floating in and out for almost thirty-two hours."

The news stunned her. How could you lose a night, a day, and another night, and never be aware of it?

"What's wrong with me?" she asked cautiously.

He sighed. "We've had this conversation before."

"I don't remember. I don't remember talking with you at all, except that first night." Her heart tumbled against her ribs. "Did I—did I say anything—anything..."

"Indiscreet?" His eyes narrowed. "Is that what you mean?"

"No," she said quickly, knowing immediately that she hadn't. Instinct told her that she wouldn't still be here if she'd babbled about how she'd set out to stalk and follow L.R. Campbell. Even though she'd ended up with the wrong man, Roarke would not take kindly to knowing he'd been hunted. "No," she said again, "it's—it's just a little upsetting not to know what you've said or done for almost two days."

"Well, you'll lose more than that, if you push your luck. You have a concussion."

"I remember you telling me that. But you said it was slight."

"It is, compared to what it might have been. And you'll be fine, so long as you take it easy for a week or so."

"A week? No, that's impossible," she said, thinking of her flight back to the States on Monday.

"Yes." His voice was grim. "It is, indeed, impossible, but Mendoza says that's what it's to be, and I'm stuck with it."

Victoria flushed. "You're not 'stuck' with anything, Mr. Campbell," she said coldly as she pulled the towel from her hair and thrust her fingers into the dark locks, fluffing them away from her face. "After I'm dressed, if you'd be good enough to arrange to have a boat take me back to San Juan——"

Roarke laughed coldly. "Oh, yes," he said softly, "I'm just about to do that, aren't I? Let you take a bumpy car ride, and then a long boat ride, so you can get ashore and suddenly develop symptoms you never had while you were here, symptoms you and some fast-talking attorney conjure up between you."

She stared at him. "I'd never——"

"No. You'd never, because I'm not going to give you the chance." He stalked across the room, snatched her clothing from the back of a chair, then dropped it on to the bed beside her. "Now, get dressed. Constancia has your breakfast ready."

"I'll get dressed when I'm good and ready. And I don't want breakfast," she said. Her voice trembled a little. "I don't want anything from you."

She cried out as he bent and caught hold of her shoulders. The pressure of his hands was harsh, but not as harsh as the way he looked at her.

"Don't argue with me," he said warningly.

"Or?" she said defiantly, forcing her eyes to meet his.

His hands tightened on her. "Or," he said in a voice so soft it was almost a whisper, "I'll strip that robe off you and dress you myself."

Victoria's heart thudded against her ribs. "Never," she said with amazing calmness.

One hand lifted from her shoulder, curved around her neck, then slipped to the back of her head. His fingers threaded into her hair, and he tilted her face up to his.

"But I've already dressed you once before," he said silkily. "It would be no trouble at all to do it again—especially now that you're awake."

The image came to her again, more clearly this time. She, awakening in the small hours of the night, sud-

denly shaking with a chill; Roarke, slipping off his shirt,
pulling down the blankets, putting his shirt around her,
his hands moving lightly across her flesh . . .

Waves of color beat into her cheeks. "Turn your
back," she said stiffly.

Roarke looked at her a moment longer, and then he
laughed and did as she'd asked, his arms folded arro-
gantly across his chest.

"As you like."

Victoria's hands shook as she unbelted the robe, then
pulled on her clothing as quickly as she could manage.
What she'd like, she thought, was to get off this island.
And that was exactly what she would do, as soon as she
could—and if Roarke Campbell didn't care for the idea,
he could just go to hell.

When she was dressed, he helped her down to the dining
room, where he deposited her at the table. Constancia
bustled in and greeted her with a broad smile.

"*Buenos días, señorita.* It is good to see you awake.
What would you like for breakfast?"

"I'm not really hungry, Constancia."

"She'll have toast," Roarke said. "And poached eggs.
And some fruit."

"But I don't want——"

"So long as you're in my charge, you will do what I
think best."

"Yes. Well, the sooner that's ended, the better."

Roarke poured two cups of coffee from a carafe on
the sideboard. "If you follow orders, you should be here
no more than a week."

Victoria put her hands in her lap, laced her fingers
tightly together, and smiled venomously.

"I really can't impose on you for that long," she said
sweetly.

It was lost on him.

"You've already imposed on me," he said bluntly. "Another few days aren't going to change that."

"Well, there are other considerations."

"Such as?"

"I'm flying home on Monday. And——"

"Monday?" His voice fairly purred. "Then why were you at Campbell's just a few days ago, looking for a job?"

What a stupid thing to have said. Think, Victoria, *think*. "Because—because I thought I'd stay in Puerto Rico for a few months, if I could."

Roarke leaned back against the sideboard and lifted his coffee cup to his mouth. Steam rose from the dark liquid, pluming across his face.

"Just like that?"

She shrugged. "Yes," she said calmly, "just like that."

"What about your family? Your job?" He paused. "Surely there's someone waiting for your return."

"Only Bernie." That much was true enough, and it almost made her smile. "And he can replace me easily."

"That's an interesting assessment of your importance," Roarke said, putting the cup down and folding his arms across his chest. His voice was tinged with a hint of derision.

Victoria fixed him with a cool look. "I'm sorry to disappoint you, but Bernie is my boss. I'm a waitress. Believe me, it wouldn't be very hard for him to find someone to take my place."

Roarke said nothing. Instead, he stepped away from the sideboard, turned his back to her, and walked to the far side of the room.

"Good." His voice was brisk. "Then your staying on here won't inconvenience anyone."

"Except you."

He swung toward her. "There's really no choice, is there?"

"Yes. There is." Her head lifted. "Have your attorney draw up some kind of statement, and I'll sign it."

His brows drew together. "What are you talking about?"

"I'm talking about the legal ramifications that have upset you so much, Mr. Campbell. I'll be more than happy to sign something that says the accident was my fault entirely."

"A release," he said with some amusement.

She nodded. "That's right. Once I've done that——"

"Either you're very naive or very clever, Victoria. A release isn't worth the paper it's written on. Even the most incompetent lawyer could invalidate it by claiming you'd still been suffering the effects of concussion when you wrote it. Or, perhaps, that I'd intimidated you." His lips drew back from his teeth. "I seem to remember you accusing me of just that the first time we met."

Victoria's spine had been stiffening as he spoke, and now she lifted her head and looked straight at him.

"Just who do you think you are, Roarke Campbell?" Her voice trembled with indignation. "You may own this island, but that doesn't make you emperor."

A cool smile twisted across his lips. "Suppose I said that it does?"

He's challenging you, Victoria, a little voice whispered within her. Let it pass—you can't beat him at this game. You can't even match him. But then she looked at that arrogant smile, at those dark, cold eyes, and she knew that she could not let him win so easily.

"It's what I know," she said evenly. "Puerto Rico is governed by the laws of the United States, it——"

He was beside her before the words had finished leaving her mouth, his hands cupping her shoulders as he lifted her to her feet.

"There is no law on Isla de la Pantera except *my* law," he said harshly. His grasp tightened when she tried to pull free. "Do you understand?"

A *frisson* of fear rippled along her skin. He was not a man to cross, she had known that from the start. But how could she let him do this to her? She had a will of her own, she was not his property.

It was the sudden darkening of his eyes that told her she'd spoken the last words aloud.

"Everything on this island is my property," he said.

"Not me," she said quickly. "Not——"

"Everything," he repeated, and his mouth dropped to hers. His hands slipped up her throat to her face, framing it so that she couldn't escape the kiss no matter how desperately she struggled.

But she wouldn't struggle. She wouldn't give him the satisfaction. She had fought against Craig, once she'd realized where all his soft caresses were leading, and what good had it done her?

"You can't fight me," he whispered, drawing back a little, enough so that she could see the darkness in his eyes. "Do you understand?"

"Yes," she said. Her voice trembled. "Oh, yes, I understand that you're stronger than I am."

He laughed. "That's right. And a hell of a lot nastier." His eyes swept over her face. "Don't make this week more difficult than it has to be, Victoria, not for either one of us."

Angry tears scalded her eyes. "I hate you," she hissed.

He laughed again, this time more softly. "Do you?" he said, and he bent down to her and kissed her again. But his mouth was soft and persuasive this time, moving on hers, enticing her to kiss him back. The heat of his body engulfed her; she felt a spiraling weakness and she shuddered against him. Roarke shifted her closer to him, his hands swept down her shoulders, down her spine to her buttocks, and he brought her against him.

"Open to me," he whispered, and suddenly she wanted to, she wanted to feel his tongue in her mouth, feel his hands on her skin.

She made a little moaning sound, desperation and something far darker mixed together, and she felt the sudden hardening of his body against hers.

"Yes," he said, his voice thick, and Victoria raised her hands to his chest. She caught his shirt in her fingers, felt the thunder of his heart beneath her palms—and then his hands cupped her shoulders again and he put her from him.

Victoria swayed dizzily. "Roarke?" she whispered—and then her lashes lifted and she looked into his face.

A wrenching coldness drove through her. He was watching her narrowly; there was no desire in his eyes, nor even the shine of sexual arousal.

Her stomach rose into her throat. What Roarke had done to her had been coldly deliberate. It had to do with domination, not passion. He had shown her, in the most elemental way, that this kingdom, and everything in it, was his.

"You bastard," she hissed, and she hit him as hard as she could, not with the flat of her hand but with her fist. The blow caught him on the mouth, hard enough to rock his head back, and a slender thread of blood bloomed on his lips.

His hand clamped around her wrist, hard enough so that she felt the pressure of his fingers on the bones, but she held her ground, her head high, waiting for whatever retaliation he might choose. Slowly, one hand still clasping her, he reached into his pocket, drew out a handkerchief, and wiped it across his mouth. He looked at the crimson stain, bright against the snowy linen.

"Do you always dance right up to the edge, Victoria?" he said softly.

Suddenly, a sound drifted through the house, carrying down the staircase and into the dining room. It was a soft sound, and yet it was enough to pierce Victoria's heart.

It was the sound of a child's voice.

Her face paled. "Who is that?" she whispered.

Roarke stuffed the handkerchief into his pocket. "Constancia?" His voice rose. "Constancia!"

The housekeeper hurried into the dining room with a heavily laden tray in her hand. "I am here, *señor*."

"Stay with Miss Hamilton." He gave Victoria a quick, cold look. "See to it she eats something."

The housekeeper nodded. "Ah, *sí*, she must if she is to get well."

They were talking about her as if she wasn't there, Victoria knew; but it didn't really matter. Every fiber of her being was centered on that one faint cry. After Roarke left the room, she looked at Constancia.

"Was that—that was a child, wasn't it?"

"*Sí*."

The answer didn't register. She was too upset.

"Here?" she said foolishly. "In this house?"

"Of course." Constancia smiled sadly as she set down the tray. "Such a pretty little one. The *señor* has not mentioned her to you?"

Victoria shook her head. "No. No, he hasn't." She hesitated. "Is it—is it his child? Señor Campbell's, I mean."

The older woman's brows rose. "Of course."

"But—you said he wasn't married."

"I said that he had no wife, *señorita*."

"I don't understand."

The housekeeper sighed dramatically. "Señor Roarke and his wife are divorced."

Victoria leaned forward. "What happened, Constancia?"

The woman's eyes darted to the door. "I should not talk out of turn," she said, but her expression was eager as she sank into the chair beside Victoria. "How could the marriage last?" she whispered, "when that one is so cold, *sí*? Like ice. No feelings, no love in the heart."

Victoria stared at her. "What do you mean?"

Constancia shrugged expressively. "I mean what I say, *señorita*. No love for anyone—not even for that innocent child. I have never seen such—how do you say it?—such emptiness in a person." She leaned closer, and her voice dropped even lower. "Sex," she said, her face distorted with disgust. "That, yes. And the knowledge to charm when it is useful. But it is all false, it is only meant for gain." She sighed and put her hand to her bosom. "*Santa Maria*, how my heart breaks for that poor little one——"

"Constancia." Roarke's voice was frigid. The housekeeper paled, shoved back her chair, and leapt to her feet.

"*Sí, señor.*"

"Surely you have better things to do than gossip."

"I am sorry. I was only——"

"I know what you were 'only,'" he said, his voice warping the word with anger. "You were 'only' interfering, as you so often seem to do."

"It was my fault," Victoria said quickly. "I asked her——"

"If you have questions, ask them of me." His voice was sharp. "Not of my staff. Is that clear?" She nodded, and he started to walk to the door. Halfway there, he stopped and turned back. "Mendoza will be by later in the afternoon. Until then, I suggest you get some rest."

"All right."

His brows rose. "No argument?"

She shook her head. "No argument. I mean—what choice do I have?"

"That's the first intelligent thing you've said since you opened your eyes this morning." He fixed her with a cold look. "My staff are at your disposal—but I've made it clear to all of them that you are not to leave this island. Understood?"

Victoria nodded, then sank back in her chair as he strode from the room. Roarke didn't have to worry about her trying to leave Isla de la Pantera, not any more.

She had to find out if it was her child whose voice she'd heard. If her baby was here, in this cold, cold house, with no mother, with only a father who was, by his housekeeper's own admission, a man with no heart, then all bets were off.

She'd take her baby and leave, and no man could stop her.

CHAPTER FIVE

"*BUENOS DÍAS*, SEÑORITA HAMILTON." Constancia smiled at Victoria as she set a platter of sliced oranges, mangoes, and bananas on the terrace dining table. "You look rested this morning. Are you feeling better?"

Victoria smiled in return. "Thank you, Constancia. I am feeling better, yes."

"That is good." The housekeeper poured a stream of coffee into a white mug and put it in front of Victoria. "The *señor* will be pleased to see how smoothly your recovery goes when he returns."

Victoria's smile dimmed. "Will he be back today, do you think?"

"Oh, *sí*, I am certain of it. By tonight, I would imagine." Constancia whisked imaginary crumbs from the glass tabletop. "Is there anything else you would like?"

"No. No, thank you. I'm just going to have some breakfast and then go for a walk along the beach."

"No swimming, *señorita*. Please, there is a strong current, and you are still weak——"

It was an admonition that Victoria had heard yesterday. Today she knew how to respond.

"No swimming," she said easily.

Constancia nodded. "To lie on the sand will be good for you. The sun will bake your bones, and the sea air will put the roses back into your cheeks. If you wish someone to accompany you——"

"I'll be fine," Victoria said quickly.

The woman smiled. "*Sí*, I think that is the truth. We will see you at lunchtime, then. I will make you a salad and an omelet, and some *flan*, perhaps."

Victoria laughed. "Either a salad or an omelet, please, and definitely not the custard. As it is my clothes barely fit after only two days."

Constancia paused at the door. "You are too thin," she said promptly. "A little weight will not hurt."

Victoria sighed as the door closed after her. The housekeeper fussed over her like a mother hen, partly out of her own concern, partly because of the orders Roarke had handed down before he'd flown off in a helicopter the evening before last. But at least there were ways to get around Constancia's well-meant interference. When Roarke returned tonight, things would be different.

Roarke Campbell was an arrogant, imperious bastard. The way he'd treated her was proof enough of that. As for that moment in his arms, when the earth had fallen away from beneath her feet—well, she'd had plenty of time to think during the past two days. What had happened was completely understandable. She had concussion, her reactions and emotions were all skewed. Roarke—damn him to hell—knew it. And he'd taken full, and brutal, advantage of her muzzy state to impress her with his power over her.

She *had* been muzzy. Very. So much so that, for a crazy little while, she'd even been positive that the child she'd heard crying was hers.

Victoria smiled wryly. But the child wasn't. It hadn't taken any clever detective work to come up with that information, either. She'd simply walked into the kitchen, taken a deep breath, and asked Constancia straight out if the *señor's* little girl was adopted.

The housekeeper had looked at her as if the blow to her head had affected her brain.

"Adopted? *La chica?* No, *señorita*; she is very much a Campbell." Sadness had softened her dark eyes. "The poor little one. It is sad to come into this world so unwanted."

Victoria leaned back in her chair and sighed. Yes, she thought, it was, indeed. The baby had been deserted by her mother and she might as well have been by her father. As far as Roarke Campbell was concerned, the child was invisible. Victoria had not heard her, except for that first day, and there'd been no sign of her since.

It seemed sad, to keep a child bottled up in the nursery. There was a uniformed nanny to care for her; Victoria had seen the woman a few times and she'd tried to speak to her, but the woman spoke only Spanish.

The only real mystery about Roarke Campbell's daughter was why his wife had abandoned her. But even that had a probable explanation. Maybe the baby was a pawn in a complicated divorce settlement. It was sad to contemplate, but such things happened all the time.

Victoria sighed again as she watched the play of sunlight on the tangle of bougainvillaea that grew along the perimeter of the terrace. Whatever was going on, it had nothing to do with her. She had to concentrate on getting well enough to convince Roarke that he could safely let her go in another five days—and not go crazy while she waited for the time to pass.

A flock of parakeets swooped overhead suddenly, their plumage as brilliant as jewels. They were beautiful birds, and her first sight of them had brought her great pleasure. Now they brought only a wistful tug to her heart. That was because Juan, Roarke's elderly gardener, had proudly explained the flock's origins to her.

"It was Señor Campbell who had them brought to Isla de la Pantera, *señorita*."

"They're not native to the island, then?" she'd asked. The old man had shaken his head. "But what keeps them here? If they're not really from this place, I mean. Why don't they fly away?''

Juan had looked at her as if she were a foolish child. "The island is beautiful, no?"

"Yes, but——"

"The birds have everything they could want. Here, they are safe, they are well cared for. Why should they leave?"

"But what if they wished to leave despite all that?" Victoria had insisted, as if there were some hidden meaning to their conversation.

Juan had shrugged his shoulders as he dug his hoe into the rich soil and stepped down on it.

"They do not try. Isla de la Pantera is too far from the main island for their fragile wings. They would not make it over the sea." He'd looked up at her and smiled. "But it does not matter. They do not choose to——"

"They *cannot* choose, you mean," she'd said, her voice sharp. "The birds are prisoners here."

The old man had laughed as the parakeets swooped across the garden, tittering and chirping to each other.

"Do they look like prisoners, *señorita*?"

No, she thought now, as she watched the tiny, feathered jewels settle on the lawn; they didn't. But they were, they were captives the same as she was. Stone walls do not a prison make, some poet or other had said, and until two days ago Victoria had never known how right he was.

She put down her cup, blotted her lips with a creamy linen napkin, and rose to her feet. There was no sense in trying to take her breakfast dishes inside. Constancia would only look at her as if she'd committed some terrible crime and launch into a gentle lecture, the gist of which was that the *señor* had left specific orders about her welfare.

Her mouth turned down as she walked slowly toward the wide brick steps that led down from the terrace. What the *señor* had left, she thought bitterly, were instructions for the care and feeding of Isla de la Pantera's newest zoological exhibit. But in five more days, she thought as she stepped on to lush lawn, she would be free.

Victoria raised her face to the sun and closed her eyes, breathing in the mingled scents of sea and tropical foliage.

"*Buenos días, señorita*. It is a lovely day, no?"

She blinked her eyes open. It was the maid. Lucia, she thought, or perhaps Anna. There were so many servants it was hard to keep track of who was who and who did what.

"Yes," she said politely. "It certainly is."

"May I get you something, *señorita*? A cold drink, perhaps, or——"

"Nothing," Victoria said quickly, following the somewhat sharply spoken word with a reassuring smile. "I don't need a thing. Honestly."

The girl smiled. "If you do——"

"If I do, I'll let you know."

"*Bueno*. I will be on my way, then, *señorita*."

Victoria nodded. Her lips felt stiff with smiling; as soon as she entered the thick rhododendron bushes that marked the boundaries of the garden, her mouth went lax.

She had, for the past two days, been waited on hand and foot, her every need attended to. Someone made her bed in the morning, turned it down at night, laid out her clothes—and she had her clothes, all of them. Later that first day, after Roarke had so graphically made clear that she was his to do with as he chose, he'd sent his helicopter pilot to her.

"If you'll give me the name of your hotel, *señorita*," he'd said politely, "I'll take a quick run to San Juan and pick up your luggage."

The luggage of Señorita Victoria Winters, she'd thought immediately. How would she get around that? The answer had been surprisingly simple.

"Fine," she'd said without blinking an eye. "Let me just phone the Mariposa and tell them to have my things waiting at the reception desk. Oh—I'll have them tag it 'Isla de la Pantera,' so that there won't be any confusion about what's mine."

The little subterfuge had worked like a charm, and a few hours later her things had been delivered to the island. And, naturally, all her clothing had been pressed and put neatly away by one of the servants.

Enjoy all this luxury, she kept telling herself. After all, she'd never known such pampering. When she was little, her mother had been too weary at the end of the long day to lavish anything but the most cursory attendance on her. And the last few years, between caring for her mother and working at the Route 66 Roadside Café, luxury had been a once-a-week hot bath in lieu of her daily quick shower.

But she couldn't enjoy it. For one thing, it seemed sybaritic to lie around, doing nothing, when everyone around her was gainfully occupied. For another— Victoria sighed as she sank down on a marble bench in the garden. For another, she was just plain bored.

She'd almost said that to Constancia a few minutes ago. But how could she? There was something contemptible about saying such a thing to the woman who spent the day waiting on you. It smacked of the sort of pomposity Victoria had despised when she was growing up, and the women her mother had worked for, whose floors she'd scrubbed and kitchens she'd cleaned, and who had sent her home with leftover food their own families were tired of, or clothing they'd no longer wear because it was out of fashion.

She rose slowly and began walking along the curving path that wound through the garden to the sloping beach that was the southern boundary of Isla de la Pantera.

"Just concentrate on getting well, *señorita*," Constancia kept saying, as if it were a magical incantation. Victoria's mouth narrowed. It probably was, in a way. Roarke must have drummed the need for her complete recovery into his staff. The sooner she was better, the sooner he could safely get rid of her. Well, the feeling was mutual. It couldn't be soon enough.

Ahead, the sunlight glinted on a white sand beach. Victoria slipped out of her sandals, then stripped down to her swimsuit, leaving her shorts and cotton T-shirt lying in a little heap beside a patch of beach grass. Sand kicked from her heels as she ran into the frothing surf. The water was warm, almost hot from the steady blaze of the sun. It curled around her calves and then her thighs like silk, and she felt the tension begin to drain from her body. Don't swim, Constancia had warned, and the doctor, too.

"No strenuous activity," he'd said sternly. "Not until you are completely well."

But swimming wasn't strenuous, especially not if she just floated on her back and let herself ride on the gentle swells, as she'd done yesterday. She rolled her shoulders as the water lapped at her breasts. God, it felt wonderful. No prying eyes, no one to tell her what she should and should not do...

"Damn it, woman! What in God's name are you up to now?" Roarke's voice roared across the silence. Victoria gasped and spun around just in time to see him come splashing into the surf fully dressed, his face twisted in rage.

"Get away from me," she yelled. "Do you hear me, Roarke? Get——"

She turned and dived into deeper water, kicking furiously, but he was too fast for her. He caught her easily and drew her back against him, his arms enclosing her just beneath her breasts, so tightly that she could feel the hammer of his heart against her back.

"You little fool. What are you trying to do, kill yourself?"

Victoria slammed her hands against his forearms. "Let go of me, damn it!"

Roarke turned her toward him. "What I ought to do," he said grimly, "is lock you in your room. That's the only way I can be sure you'll behave yourself."

"I *was* behaving myself. In fact, I was having a perfectly lovely time, until you——"

"Mendoza told you not to do anything strenuous. And Constancia warned you about the currents."

Victoria tossed the wet hair from her face. "It must be wonderful to be God," she snapped.

Roarke's brows rose. "And what is that supposed to mean?"

"Just what it sounds like." Her jaw shot forward. "Tell me, do you know all this because you can see it when you look down from Mount Olympus, or is it just that your watchdogs report in every hour, on the hour?"

He stared at her, and then a tight smile curved across his mouth.

"Watchdogs?" he asked softly. "Is that how you would describe people who are concerned about your welfare?"

"Correction," she said coldly. "*Your* welfare. After all, we all want to make certain *señor* doesn't end up with a seriously injured woman on his hands. She might sue for a billion trillion dollars!"

Roarke sighed. "Come on," he said, slipping his arm around her shoulders. "Let's get out of the water and into dry——"

"Thank you," she said, stepping free of his encircling arm as they reached the sandy beach, "but I'm comfortable just the way I am." She glared at him. "What are you doing here, anyway? Constancia said you wouldn't be back until tonight."

His eyes glinted with sudden amusement. "How could I stay away a minute longer than necessary, when I knew you were pining for my return?"

"The only thing I pine for is my departure from this place."

Roarke smiled. "Constancia was right. She said it was obvious you were feeling much better, because you were prickly as a pincushion."

"I am not prickly. I am just—just tired of being treated like an invalid."

"But you are an invalid, Victoria. You had a bad blow to the head, and you need to take it easy for a bit." His arms looped around her shoulders again and he turned toward the sloping sand dune. "Now let's see about some dry clothing and a cup of tea, and——"

She spun toward him, her face flushed and raised to his. "Damn it, Roarke——"

He cupped her shoulders and stepped back from her. "All right, then, let's see how you look. Constancia says your color's better, and she's managed to put some flesh on your bones."

"My color's fine," she said stiffly. "And I don't need any flesh on my bones. I——"

She broke off in bewilderment as he looked at her, working his way slowly from her face to her toes, then up again. Her swimsuit was a one piece, cut for serviceability and not fashion, but she suddenly felt as if she were standing naked before him. A tingly sensation spread along her body, as if she'd touched something and got a low electric shock.

"Much better color," he said softly, his gaze steady on her face. His eyes dropped a little, and to her horror she felt her breasts lift, the nipples thrusting tightly against the thin nylon of her suit.

"Are you done?" Her voice trembled a little as she wrapped her arms around herself.

Roarke laughed softly as his gaze returned to her face. "What is it, Victoria? Are you cold?"

"Yes. I am. But I'm not going back to the house," she added defiantly. "I'm going for a walk." She tossed the last remark over her shoulder as she set off along the beach at a brisk pace, but she hadn't got very far before Roarke fell in beside her.

She glanced at him out of the corner of her eye. He'd pulled off his wet shirt and shoes, and now he was dressed only in soaked, skintight faded jeans. His body was golden in color, lean and tightly muscled. Dark, silken hair lay in whorls across his chest, then arrowed down to his low waistband.

The electric awareness danced along her skin again, and she swept her gaze straight ahead.

"I don't need company, thank you," she said briskly.

"How have you been feeling?"

"We did this already, remember? You've had a full report from Mendoza and Constancia, and probably from every other flunky in your——"

She cried out as he clasped her shoulders hard and swung her toward him.

"Answer the question." His face was set in cold, unyielding lines. "How do you feel?"

"I told you——"

"Then tell me again."

Victoria puffed out her breath. "I feel fine."

"Mendoza says you still get headaches."

"Occasionally."

"Are you still seeing double?"

She wrenched away from him. "No. You can stop worrying. My recovery is uneventful."

A hint of a smile touched Roarke's lips. "That sounds like a quote from Mendoza."

"It is. He checks me twice a day." She began walking, and Roarke fell in beside her. "He lives on the island, too, doesn't he?"

"Yes. He has a home on the other side." Roarke bent down and scooped up a tiny whelk shell. "He's quite competent, in case you were concerned."

"It never occurred to me he'd be anything less," she said frankly. "I'm just surprised you'd share your little bit of paradise with him."

Roarke drew back his arm and tossed the shell into the sea. "The arrangement suits us both. Mendoza is from New York. We met a few years ago. His wife had been taken ill, and he'd brought her to the islands to recover. He was trying his damnedest to figure a way to resettle in a warm climate without retiring completely."

"So you offered him the chance to be Roarke Campbell's personal physician."

Roarke shook his head. "I offered him the chance to set up a small clinic on Isla de la Pantera. I'd just bought it, but I knew I'd end up with a fair-size community."

"What do you mean?"

"Well, you've seen how many people there are on the staff."

"How many you need to keep that enormous house running smoothly for its lord and master, you mean? Yes."

"I hate to disappoint you, Victoria, but most of those people were here when I took over, and I'd no intention of displacing them. Besides, they provide useful services. We raise goats and chickens, there's quite a large vegetable farm, there's even a couple of fishing boats that dock in the harbor.'' He shrugged his shoulders. ''It made sense to have decent medical care available for me and my people.''

That wasn't quite the way Victoria had imagined it, but she wasn't about to give Roarke anything.

''All that,'' she said with faint derision, ''just so you can escape the mean streets of San Juan.''

''All that,'' he said evenly, ''so I can get away from the pressure cooker world where I earn my bread, and live a quiet life part of the time. But I suppose that sounds deadly dull to you.''

She looked at him. ''Why do you say that?''

''Constancia says you've been fidgety. She says you're obviously bored. She says——''

''Has it ever occurred to you that I might be the best person to ask about me?'' Victoria stopped walking and swung around to face him.

Roarke's brows lifted. ''I've tried that, remember? You keep saying that you're fine.''

''I am. I mean, I'm recovering from the accident.'' She took a deep breath. ''But I'm bored to death.''

His mouth thinned. ''Yes. That's what I thought. An island with no television, no radio, no clubs or restaurants or theatres must be dull as hell for——''

''There's nothing dull about peace and serenity, Roarke.''

His eyes fixed on hers. ''No?''

Victoria pushed her damp hair from her face. ''No. I'm bored because no one will let me do anything.''

''I left orders that——''

''I know. And that's the trouble.'' She threw her arms wide. ''I'm going crazy. I'm not used to doing nothing hour after hour.''

Roarke folded his arms against his chest. "And what would you like to do?" A taut smile twisted over his mouth. "Paint? Sculpt? Take up Swahili?"

"How about making my own bed, for openers? Or making my own toast for breakfast? Or even laying out my own nightgown——?"

"Ah, that's too bad," he said, his smile widening. "The lady wears nightgowns, and here I've been imagining her in my shirts all this time."

"The point is," Victoria said quickly, "I'm perfectly capable of doing something useful."

"Yes," Roarke said quietly, his smile fading. "I'm sure you are. But I don't need a cook or a maid, I don't need a housekeeper——"

"Well, you certainly need someone to take care of your daughter."

Her eyes widened as she realized what she'd said. It was as unplanned as it was unexpected, but as soon as the words left her mouth, she knew that the idea had been tumbling around in the back of her mind for the past two days. Here she was, aching for a child she'd never seen, and there she was, Roarke's daughter, no doubt properly fed and clothed and all the rest, but lacking the love she deserved.

Roarke was looking at her as if she'd suggested the sea might be convinced to stop beating against the sand.

"And what exactly is that supposed to mean?" he said coldly.

Victoria swallowed against the sudden dryness in her mouth. "I've seen her nanny——"

"Emilia."

"Whatever her name is. And—I'm sure she's competent. But she hasn't done anything with your baby for the past two days. She hasn't even had her out of the house..." Victoria paused and drew in her breath. "Why are you looking at me like that?"

Roarke's expression grew grim. "For a woman who's so certain she knows everything there is to know about me," he said quietly, "you really know remarkably little."

"Look, I'm not criticizing you."

"Aren't you?" His tone was silken.

"I just thought, as long as I'm going to be here another couple of days——"

"You just thought, since the evil emperor had locked his child away in the castle, you would set her free."

Victoria flushed. "No. I mean——"

"Your arrogance is appalling, Victoria. I'm King Midas. And you——" He reached out and clasped her wrists. "You," he said, drawing her toward him, "are Lady Bountiful, bored with life and willing to amuse herself by playing with dolls."

"It isn't like that at all. I—I like children." Victoria's mouth trembled. "It—it hurts me to think of a child being lonely, wanting love or attention or—or——"

"Daddy!"

Roarke looked over Victoria's shoulder. His face changed instantly, the dark scowl replaced by a smile so dazzling that it transformed him completely, just as it had that morning in the elevator, when he'd smiled at her for the first time.

"Susanna."

Victoria turned as Roarke let go of her, and her heart almost leaped from her breast. The Spanish nanny was standing a few yards down the beach, smiling pleasantly—and she was holding a child in her arms.

The woman said something in rapid Spanish. Roarke answered just as quickly, and then he dropped to his knees and held out his arms as the nanny lowered the child to the sand. Susanna raced to him, her little face beaming, and he caught her and swung her high over his head as he got to his feet.

"Hello, sweetheart. Did you think I wasn't coming back to get you?"

The nanny said something again, and Roarke nodded. "She's right," he said to Victoria, "I should have brought Susanna down to the beach with me and introduced you properly." He grinned as he seated the child on his shoulders. "Susu, this is Victoria. Can you say hello?"

Roarke's daughter giggled. "'Lo, Toria."

Say something, Victoria told herself furiously. Say something, and stop staring at that dark hair and those blue eyes. Why wouldn't she look like that? Roarke's hair is dark, his eyes are gray...

"It's your fault Susanna thought I'd deserted her," Roarke said.

Victoria blinked and looked at him. He was watching her narrowly, his face devoid of expression.

"I—I'm sorry. What did you say?"

"I said, my desertion's your fault, Victoria. Emilia whisked Susu off for a bath and a nap after our helicopter ride. I promised I'd come up and tuck her in." A teasing light danced in his eyes. "But I got delayed, rescuing you."

"You didn't rescue me. I was doing just fine, until you——" Victoria stared at him. "What helicopter ride?"

Roarke set the child down and patted her bottom gently, and she ran up the beach to Emilia.

"The one that brought us back from San Juan. Well, from Miami, actually. But——"

"You mean—you mean Susanna was with you? She wasn't here while you were gone on business?"

Roarke smiled. "What a script you've written, Victoria," he said gently. "Big, bad Roarke Campbell, heartless capitalist..."

"Wait a minute. I didn't——"

"...heartless capitalist, flies off to make millions while his infant daughter languishes, unloved, in his castle." His mouth thinned. "Have I left anything out?"

"That's not—I didn't——" Argument was pointless. He was right, and they both knew it. After a moment, she nodded her head. "I'm sorry," she said softly. "Very sorry."

Roarke went on glaring at her for a few seconds longer, and then he sighed, cupped her elbow, and began walking her slowly back toward the house.

"All right, I guess I can't really blame you." He gave her a quick glance. "I suppose I did come on like the king of Isla de la Pantera the other day."

My God, she thought in amazement, was Roarke Campbell offering an apology?

"Yes," she said quietly. "You did."

"Yeah." Roarke lifted his shoulders, then let them fall. "Look, this isn't an apology——"

Victoria bit back a smile. "No," she said mildly, "I didn't imagine it would be."

"But it is an explanation." He cleared his throat. "The thing of it is, I was suspicious about you."

Her throat constricted. "Yes," she said in a small voice. "Well, I suppose—I suppose I can understand that. After all——"

Roarke caught hold of her shoulders and swung around to face her. "No," he said quietly. His eyes were very dark, and very still on hers. "No, I doubt if you could possibly understand." One hand slid to her throat and curved lightly around it. He smiled, and his thumb smoothed gently along her mouth. "I guess I *am* apologizing," he said. "We got off to a bad start. And I'd like to change that."

Victoria tipped her head up and stared at him. Her mind was whirling in tight circles, while she tried desperately to sort things out. Where was the cold, imperious Roarke Campbell she knew? For that matter, where was the unfeeling man with no heart whom Constancia had described?

"Well?" He put his hands on her shoulders again. "Do you think we could try to be friends?"

"Yes. Yes, I—I'd like that."

"Good. Then let's seal the pact." Victoria nodded and held out her hand. Roarke smiled. "There's a better way," he said softly.

She caught her breath as his dark head dipped toward hers. The brush of his lips was soft, almost hesitant, and then his mouth opened on hers. She rose on her toes and leaned toward him, and suddenly the sea and the sand spun away.

When he finally lifted his head, Victoria was trembling.

"Friends?" he said.

She didn't trust herself to speak. She nodded instead, and then she let him put his arm lightly around her shoulders and walk her slowly to the house.

CHAPTER SIX

LATE afternoon sunlight filtered into the kitchen, casting a golden light over the old-fashioned butcher-block worktable that stood in the center of the floor. The room was wrapped in a pleasant silence, broken only by the soft hum of the bees that lazed above the flowers growing in riotous profusion just outside the open door.

Constancia, who had been shelling peas into a terracotta bowl, rose from the table and walked to the sink. She turned on the water and began humming a snatch of song in a husky, somewhat off-key voice.

Victoria, who had been arranging a tumble of frangipani, bougainvillaea and periwinkles in a woven basket, looked up and smiled.

"That's a pretty tune, Constancia. What is it?"

The housekeeper laughed as she dried her hands on a linen towel. "It is pretty, *sí*, but not when I sing it, I am afraid. My musical talent leaves much to be desired." She opened the refrigerator and peered into its depths. "*La chica* is the only one in this house who truly appreciates my singing."

"Susanna, you mean." Victoria tucked the last flowers into the basket, then shifted so that she was facing Constancia. "She seems to be a very sweet child," she said softly.

Constancia nodded. *"Sí."*

"Constancia?" Victoria hesitated. "When you said those things about someone in this house being cold and heartless—you were talking about Señor Campbell's wife, weren't you?"

"*Sí.* Of course. Of who else would I say such things?"
The housekeeper rummaged around in the refrigerator
and took out a platter of freshly caught red snapper.

Victoria looked at her. "I've noticed," she said slowly,
"that Susanna never mentions her mother."

"No. Her mother left when Susanna was an infant."

It was hard to imagine, Victoria thought. Her heart
ached for a child she'd never seen, but Roarke's wife
had walked off and left her child behind.

"Has she ever been back to see Susu?"

"She has been back, *sí*, but it was not her love for
the child that brought her." Constancia wiped her hands
on her apron. "What is between the *señor* and *señora*
will never end." There was a silence, and the housekeeper looked over her shoulder and smiled. "So you
like Susu, yes? You have spent much time with her the
past days."

Victoria's smile was tremulous. "I—I like children.
And Susanna's a lovely child."

"*Sí*, she is. You are good for her, *señorita*. She flourishes like a flower under a woman's touch."

"I'm glad you think so."

"I know so." The housekeeper smiled slyly. "I know,
too, that Susu is not the only one who flourishes, yes?"

Victoria looked up in surprise. "What do you mean?"

"I mean that Señor Campbell is very happy, too."
Constancia took a knife from the rack and began honing
it on a sharpening stone. "I have not seen him this way
in a long time."

A little rush of pleasure raced through Victoria's veins.
"Really?"

The housekeeper nodded. "He laughs, he smiles—and
he comes home early every night."

"Well, I suppose he's—he's being polite."

Constancia grinned. "You think so? I think he is not
a man much given to worrying about what is polite and

what is not, *señorita*. If the Governor himself were here and Señor Campbell did not wish to talk with him, he would not do so."

Victoria laughed softly. "I suppose you're right."

"Of course I am right. To see him seated opposite you at the dining-room table every night, talking and smiling, instead of eating alone with his nose tucked into the news-paper——" The older woman sighed. "It is something I have not seen before."

Victoria touched her tongue to her lips. "Not since—since his divorce, you mean?"

Constancia's black eyes snapped. "Nor before that, either. His wife did not like to spend her evenings at home." She slammed a pan onto the gas range. "She did not deserve him, that is certain."

"Why did she leave him?"

The housekeeper's face darkened. "For another man."

Victoria stared at her. "She left Roarke for someone else? But how could she? How could she want any other man after...?" She fell silent, while a quick rush of color raced into her cheeks, and then she got quickly to her feet. "I—I think I'll take a stroll before dinner. If the *señor* should arrive early and want me——"

"What if he does?" She whirled around, and Roarke smiled at her from the doorway.

"Roarke." Victoria swallowed hard. "I didn't—I didn't hear you come in. How long have you been standing there?"

"Only a couple of seconds." He smiled again. "I hated to break up this domestic scene. I hope Constancia hasn't let you overdo things."

"No. No, she barely lets me lift a finger."

God! Her tongue seemed too thick to manage normal speech. Had he heard that foolish slip of hers? She didn't think so, but then, why was he looking at her that way, with that little smile on his mouth? If only she hadn't said something so ridiculous. What on earth had she been thinking of? Maybe it was because of the concussion. She still had an occasional headache, after all, and her eyes were——

"...black and blue."

Victoria started. "What?"

"I said, you shouldn't attempt anything taxing yet. You're still suffering the effects of that blow to the head." He frowned as he walked toward her. "Your eyes are still discolored."

"Yes, they are, a little. Dr. Mendoza says——"

"Tilt your head to the light." Roarke clasped her face in his hands and raised it. His hands were cool against her flushed skin; he was so close that she could feel his breath against her cheek. A tiny tremor went through her, and his frown deepened. "What is it?"

"Nothing," she said quickly.

"Does this hurt?"

His hand moved lightly across her skin. It was all she could do to keep from trembling.

"No," she said quickly. "No, I just—I just——" She looked at him helplessly. "Actually—actually, it's the sun. It's—it's in my eyes."

Roarke smiled as he let go of her. "That's because it's trying to tell you something."

His smile was contagious. She felt her own mouth curve in response to his.

"Is it?"

He nodded. "Yes," he said, taking her hand. "Constancia? How long until dinner?"

"Twenty minutes, no longer."

Roarke grinned. "Ah," he said. "An hour. That's just about right."

The housekeeper put her hands on her hips. "Twenty minutes, *señor.*"

"Constancia! How can I show Señorita Hamilton the most glorious sunset in the world in so short a time?"

Victoria looked at him, bewildered. "An hour? To watch the sun set?"

Roarke shook his head in dismay. "Do you see how little the woman knows of sunsets, Constancia?" He cocked his head toward the housekeeper. "What do you say?"

Constancia sighed and threw up her hands. "*Sí, bueno.* One hour." She cast a despairing glance at the red snapper, waiting in a pan beside the oven. "After that, what happens to the poor *chillo* will be on your head."

It took no time at all to realize why it was going to take an hour to watch the sun set on Isla de la Pantera. Roarke described it as a solemn old custom, although within minutes it was easy to see that whatever customs were involved were being invented, right on the spot.

They stopped first in the library, where he pulled off his jacket and tie and dumped them over the back of a chair.

"All right," he said, peering into the depths of a handsome mahogany wall unit that opened to reveal a drinks cabinet. "We'll need provisions for our trip."

Victoria laughed. "What are you talking about? What trip?"

"What do you think?" he said, ignoring her questions. "Shall it be a Rum Collins? Or a *piña colada*? Toria? What's your preference?"

"I've never had a *piña* whatever——"

"*Colada.*" He smiled at her as he took out a decanter of rum, then reached into a small refrigerator tucked discreetly into the base of the unit. "Pineapple juice, ice—now for the special Campbell magic——"

She watched, laughing, as he dumped things into a blender, then whirred them to a froth.

"There we are," he said, pouring their drinks with a flourish. "Sustenance for our journey. Are you ready, Miss Hamilton?"

"I suppose so. But where are we going?"

Roarke smiled mysteriously as he handed her a chilled glass. "On the eternal quest," he said. "We seek the perfect sunset." He touched his glass lightly to hers. "And tonight, who knows? We may just find it."

Hand in hand, laughing as they went, they made their way down the terrace and into the garden. A giant Sierra palm tree grew in its heart; by the time they reached it, its white-blossomed fruit spikes seemed to be tipped with the fire of the sun.

"The first stop on the Campbell tour," Roarke said, nodding toward the towering tree. "What do you think?"

Victoria drew in her breath. "I think it's beautiful," she said softly.

Their eyes met. There was a sudden silence, and then he smiled and tugged lightly on her hand. "Let's go," he said. "We've two more stops to make."

Victoria laughed. "Two more? But——"

"And if we're late, the show will go on without us. Lift your glass to the Sierra palm, first. That's it. Take a sip of your drink—good." His fingers laced through hers. "Okay. Next stop, the top of Panther Mountain."

The mountain was really little more than a gentle slope that rose in the center of Isla de la Pantera. There was a narrow, grassy trail curving up to the top, and by the time they reached what Roarke laughingly called the summit, the sun hung suspended over the sea, turning the high, puffy clouds that always floated over the island to crimson and gold.

"Oh, Roarke." Victoria's voice was barely a whisper. "How beautiful."

His arm slid around her shoulders. "It is, isn't it? I think I could live here for a thousand years and never grow tired of this view." He pointed out across the sea. "In the fall, if you're lucky, you can see the storms blowing in across the Caribbean, like dark shadows over the land."

"I've never seen anything like it," she said slowly. "I feel as if I can see forever."

He nodded. "There's only one view better." His hand clasped hers. "Come on, and I'll show it to you."

Moments later, standing barefoot in the warm sand on the beach, Victoria knew he was right. This view of the sun, lying on the rising breast of the sea, was spectacular.

"Is it always like this?" she whispered.

Roarke smiled and raised his glass in mock salute to the sky. "No, not always. Sometimes it's even more brilliant."

She smiled in return. "Now I know why you bought Isla de la Pantera."

"For the sunsets?" He laughed softly. "Actually, there were two reasons."

"What was the other?"

He squeezed her shoulder lightly. "The sunrises."

Victoria smiled. "Why do I get the feeling you're not really joking?"

Roarke took her empty glass and set it down with his, on the sand, and then they began walking slowly along the beach, their bare feet in the warm surf.

"The truth is that buying the island started out as a business venture. I'd seen too many small islands snatched up and badly developed in this part of the world, and I thought the future—the real future—lay in learning to create communities on these islands that would draw tourists while not compromising the environment."

"Sounds impossible."

"Not impossible—but tough. Very tough. Anyway, I commissioned a guy to take aerial photographs of the area for me as part of a deal, when I came across the shots of Isla de la Pantera."

Victoria glanced at him and nodded. "Island of the Panther."

Roarke smiled. "Your Spanish is improving, hmm?"

She laughed and shook her head. "I asked Constancia what it meant. She said it was not named for a black leopard but for a mystical jaguar."

"Very mystical." He smiled again. "Considering that jaguars and leopards don't exist on these islands, and never have."

"Why the name, then?"

Roarke slipped his arm around her shoulders. "No one is certain, but it's probably tied up with voodoo."

"Voodoo? Are you kidding?"

"Cross my heart. Lots of people in the Caribbean practice voodoo—including some of the ones who live on this island. They have some sort of legend about a solitary creature—half man, half jaguar—who roams these hills." He gestured across the low dunes, toward the interior of the island, where darkness had already overtaken the dwindling daylight. "He lives here, alone, the legend says, because he can't find peace anywhere else."

Victoria glanced at Roarke from beneath her lashes. The fading light played across his face, painting his high cheekbones with shadow.

"How sad," she said softly.

He nodded. "Yes." His voice was tight. "I thought so, too. I flew out to take a look at the island—and I knew I had to have it."

"So you bought it."

"It took a while. The government didn't want to sell it to me—they already had plans for a casino and apartment blocks." She felt his fingers flex, then tighten on her shoulder. "And there were others who were opposed—who thought my plans for the island would keep it too isolated to be of any value."

"But they were wrong."

He laughed softly. "Who knows what's right or wrong in this life, Victoria? I think the island is beyond value." His smile twisted. "But there are those who would disagree, who would tell you that living here, in such a primitive setting, away from everything else..."

His voice faded away, just as the sun fell behind the horizon. Victoria looked at him, at the downward curve of his mouth, and she knew that he was talking about his wife.

"Roarke?" She drew a deep breath. "When you bought the island—did you know then how your wife felt about it?"

He came to a stop, so sudden and abrupt that she almost stumbled.

"What kind of question is that?"

The harshness in his voice stung her. She couldn't see his face clearly, now that the sun was almost gone, but she knew how it must look: cold, hard, unyielding.

"I just—I wondered how—I mean, Constancia said——"

She broke off, swallowing her words, wishing she had thought before she'd spoken.

"Constancia's turning into an old woman who has nothing better to do than gossip. What did she tell you?"

"Nothing. Well, just that your wife didn't like the island."

His laughter was without humor. "An understatement, Victoria. She despised it."

"And that you and she—that you're divorced."

"Yes, we are. We have been for more than two years."
He drew a harsh breath, then spoke in a cold voice. "Is
there anything else you want to know?"

"I'm sorry," she said quickly. "I—I didn't mean to
pry——"

Roarke clasped her tightly. "I have no wish to discuss
Alexandra," he said grimly. "Do I make myself clear?"

Victoria nodded. "Yes," she said softly.

Oh, yes, she thought, as they began walking back
toward the garden, he had made himself very clear.
Constancia was right; whatever had existed between
Roarke and his wife wasn't over yet. Alexandra. It was
an elegant, lovely name. Was the woman elegant, too?
Did he still miss her? Yes, he must. That was why he
couldn't talk about her, why...

"Toria?" Roarke slipped his arm around her waist.
"What is it?"

"Nothing. Just—I felt a chill, that's all."

"I've probably walked you too far. Shall I go back
and get the Jeep?"

"No," she said quickly. "No, I'm fine. I just—I guess
I was thinking about the jaguar. The one the island's
named after." She looked up at him and smiled. "Tell
me more about voodoo. Do the islanders still practice
it?"

"Yes. There's a plateau on the west shore, over-
looking the sea—I've seen the glow of the bonfires there,
a few times. In fact, I've been invited to attend the
ceremonies."

"And have you?"

"No, not yet." He smiled. "Why? Would you like to
watch?"

She tilted her head back and looked at him. "I don't
know," she said softly. "Although—yes. I think it would
be fascinating."

"Well, then, the next time I'm invited, I'll accept for the both of us. How does that sound?"

A delighted smile curved across her mouth. "It sounds wonderful! Are you sure they won't mind if I—oh!" Her face fell. "Thank you for asking me. But I'll be leaving the day after tomorrow."

Roarke held back the heavy branches of the rhododendron as they entered the garden.

"The day after tomorrow," he murmured. "That's right. I almost forgot."

The day after tomorrow. How could that be? It seemed impossible to think of seeing San Juan again, with its crowded streets and hotels, and the thought of Chicago, lying buried beneath the snow, was even more foreign.

She would be there, a million miles away. And Roarke—Roarke would be here; she would never see him again, she would——

"Constancia tells me you're learning Spanish."

"Yes." She cleared her throat. "At least, I've been trying. Constancia's a good teacher, but I'm afraid I still sound like a displaced mid-westerner."

All around them, thousands of tiny lights hidden in the branches of the trees blinked to life, as pale as the moon rising overhead. Roarke slowed his pace.

"Is that how you feel?" he said. "Displaced?"

Victoria shook her head. "No, not at all. Everyone's been very kind."

He stopped, caught hold of her shoulders, and turned her toward him.

"Then you don't feel as if Isla de la Pantera is a prison?"

"A prison? No. Why would you——?" A dark flush rose in her cheeks. "Juan told you what I said about the parakeets," she said slowly. When he said nothing, she smiled ruefully. "I was angry that day, I guess, and

I thought——"

"You thought, "'Aha, here's a rich man, playing at being God'''". And, in a way, you were right."

"Roarke——"

"The birds are from a species that lives in a rainforest that borders Brazil. A friend—a guy I went to school with—did his doctoral thesis on the flock. He knew they were doomed—that between the burning of the rainforest and human encroachment their population had dropped from——"

"You mean, you had them brought here to save them?"

He smiled thinly. "I'm not a complete altruist, Victoria. I brought them here because it was good for both of us, the flock and me. It saved them, and it gave me pleasure. Do you understand?"

Yes, she thought, she did. He was telling her that he was a man who took what he wanted, if it suited him, and that he did not always do things for reasons that were immediately clear.

But she knew that already. His complexity had frightened her at first; perhaps it still did. He could be moody and removed one moment, charming and warm the next. He could be demanding, almost arrogant in his single-mindedness. But he was always exciting, always filled with life...

"Toria, you really do like it here, don't you?"

She nodded. "Yes. Very much. Especially since everyone's stopped treating me like an invalid."

He smiled. "You've managed to get on Constancia's good side, I notice. Believe me, that takes some doing."

Victoria laughed. "Her bark is worse than her bite."

"Emilia tells me you've struck it off well with Susanna."

"That didn't take any effort at all. She's a wonderful little girl."

Roarke nodded. "You won't get any argument from me on that." His eyes swept over her face. "Do you like children, Victoria?"

She felt the swift, painful constriction of her heart. "I love children," she said softly.

The night breeze, softly perfumed with frangipani, blew silken strands of dark hair across her cheek. Roarke reached out and stroked them back, his fingers gentle against her skin.

"Why isn't there a man waiting for you back in— where was it?"

"Broadwell. And——" her breath caught as he cupped her face in his hands and brushed his thumbs over her cheekbones "—how do you know there isn't?"

He laughed softly. "You told me, remember? Anyway, if there were, you wouldn't have come looking for a job here."

At first, she didn't know what he meant. "What are you talking about?"

Roarke drew back and looked at her. "You said you were looking for a job the day you came bulling your way into Campbell's."

Victoria exhaled sharply. "Oh. Oh, that." She forced a little laugh. "Actually—actually, that was a spur-of-the-moment idea. I—I came here on vacation, and I took one look at the sun and the sea and I thought, Why should I go back to an Illinois winter?"

She waited, holding her breath, until finally he nodded his understanding.

"Yeah, having survived my share of northern winters, I can see that." He smiled. "Did you tell me the truth about yourself?"

Her heart turned over. "The truth?"

"Yes. Are you really a waitress?"

Her chin lifted. That was what Craig had said, in almost the same way.

"Yes," she said coolly. "Is there something wrong with being a waitress?"

"Hey." He smiled. "I was only thinking that waiting on tables is a rough job."

"Really." Her voice was as stiff as her spine.

"Really." His smile broadened. "I spent the summers of my first two years at university waiting on tables."

Victoria's brows rose. "I don't believe it."

Roarke laughed. "Adam and Eve on a raft," he sang out. "Scramble two, gimme a stack, bag a regular and a Danish."

She felt the sudden rigidity ease away. "The man speaks lunch counterese," she said lightly. "Don't tell me you come from humble beginnings."

He laughed again. "I come from lofty beginnings made humble by a father who chose not to take the business advice he paid people to provide him, but that's a whole other story." He laid his hands lightly on her shoulders. "Okay. Let me be sure I've got this all straight. You like Isla de la Pantera?"

"Yes," she said, with a puzzled smile. "I do."

"You're not terribly worried about walking out on your career."

He said it with such good humor that she had to laugh.

"You might say that, yes."

His smile grew crooked. "And you're no longer convinced I'm the world's worst villain?"

"Right." Her heart kicked against her ribs. "You might say that, too, I suppose."

"What about family, then?"

"There's no one," she said. Her voice caught, and she swallowed. "No one at all."

His expression became suddenly serious. "Well, then." He cleared his throat.

Her smile faded slowly. He was watching her with an unsettling intensity, and suddenly she felt cold.

"Well, then, what?" she asked cautiously.

"I have something to ask you, Victoria. And I want you to think carefully about your answer before you give it to me."

Her heart thudded again, but this time as accompaniment to a dizzying panic. What could he possibly want to ask her that would put such a determined look on his face? Unless—unless by some terrible twist of fate he'd found out about her, that she'd lied and cheated her way into his life, that she—that she'd given up her child...

"What is it you want to know?"

Roarke cleared his throat again. "Will you stay here, on Isla de la Pantera?"

It took a moment for his words to make sense. "What?"

"I said, how would you feel about becoming Susanna's nanny?" When she didn't answer, he smiled into her eyes. "What I'm trying to tell you is that I'd like you to stay here, Victoria. I'd like that very much."

CHAPTER SEVEN

IT WAS evening, and the nursery shutters were closed against the sun that still hung in the tropical sky. A pool of light illuminated the bentwood rocking chair where Victoria sat holding Susanna, her dark head bent over the child's, while she read softly to her.

"And the prince lifted the princess to the back of his horse..."

"An' they lived happ'ly ever after," Susu said drowsily.

Victoria smiled as she closed the well-thumbed volume of fairy tales and put it on the bedside table.

"Yes," she said, "that's right, they lived happily ever after." She smoothed back the little girl's dark curls. "Bedtime," she whispered.

The child sighed and wound her arms around Victoria's neck as she got to her feet. "Where's Teddy?"

"Teddy's right here, sweetheart. Now, you just lie down—that's the way—and I'll cover you up."

"Cover Teddy, too," Susu murmured as she snuggled under the blankets. Her feathery lashes drooped to her cheeks, then lifted. "Toria?"

"What, sweetheart?"

The child sighed again and rolled onto her belly. "Don't never go 'way," she whispered. Her eyelids closed and within seconds she was fast asleep.

Victoria watched her for a moment, her eyes dark. Then she kissed Susu's brow and shut off the bedside lamp. The room was swallowed up in darkness except for the soft illumination of the Bambi night-light plugged into the wall beside the bed.

Out in the hall, she leaned back against the wall, her throat muscles working as she tried to swallow past the lump that had risen in her throat. Dear God, she thought, help me.

What a fool she'd been to accept Roarke's offer. Why hadn't she realized it? Sighing, she made her way slowly to her bedroom and shut the door after her. The simple fact was, she hadn't wanted to realize much of anything that night. Roarke wanted her to stay, that was all that had mattered. And she'd said yes without thinking for one instant about what would come next.

No. That wasn't quite right. She *had* thought about it, and what her foolish brain had conjured up were sunny days spent caring for Susanna, and long, quiet evenings at Roarke's side.

Victoria walked to the french windows and opened them to the warm evening breeze. The trouble was, those pretty pictures hadn't been grounded in reality—a reality which she had determinedly ignored for as long as she could.

She was in Roarke's home under false pretenses. She was a liar and a cheat—a tremor went through her as she sank down onto the bench before the dressing table. She was hardly the kind of woman Roarke thought she was. The knowledge had been building inside her for days; she'd kept ignoring it, like someone who thought you could confront a demon by pretending it wasn't really there.

But last night she'd been forced to confront reality. She and Roarke had been sitting in the library reading, while a Rachmaninov piano concerto played on the compact disc player. Suddenly, Victoria had felt uneasy. When she'd looked up, she'd found Roarke watching her.

"Is something wrong?" she'd said, after a moment.

He'd smiled a little, and then his gaze had swept over her like a caress. Her skin had tingled, as if it were going to go up in flame.

"Victoria," he'd said softly.

Just that. One word—her name. But it had been filled with an intensity that matched the way he was looking at her.

Her mouth had gone dry, but somehow she'd managed a shaky smile and a foolish, breathless, "What?"

"Nothing," he'd said. "I just like the sound of your name. It suits you—did anyone ever tell you that?"

No one had. And no one had ever looked at her as if the air between them seemed to crackle.

"It—it was my grandmother's. I always thought it was sort of old-fashioned."

Roarke had smiled again. "That's why it suits you." She'd looked at him helplessly, watching as he rose slowly to his feet and started toward her, and then, with all the grace of a frightened rabbit, she'd sprung from her chair, scattering magazines across the floor while she'd mumbled something about wanting to make an early night of it, and fled.

Safe in her room, leaning back against the closed door with her heart thumping, one word had drummed inside Victoria's head with each pulse of her blood.

Liar, she'd thought, liar, liar, *liar*! And as she stared into the mirror, that was the word that leaped into her mind. That was what she was, and nothing she could say or do would change it. What would Roarke think about her sweet, old-fashioned name suiting her if he knew the truth? What would he say if he knew that she'd entered his life trying to find a baby that she'd given away—a baby that had been fathered out of wedlock by a man she'd never loved?

A sob rose in her throat and she clapped her hands to her mouth. Why hadn't she thought of all this before she'd said yes, she'd stay on as Susanna's governess.

"You were so stupid," she whispered to her reflection, and the sad-eyed woman in the mirror offered no argument. But then, she'd been stupid before. It was what had started this mess in the first place.

Victoria sighed and picked up her hairbrush, pulling it absently through the dark curls that tumbled around her face. Her hair needed cutting. It was thick and it could be unruly, as if it had a mind of its own.

Her hand stilled. That was the first thing Craig had ever said to her.

"Those pretty curls look as if they have a mind of their own," he'd said pleasantly over the Route 66 Roadside Café breakfast menu as she stood waiting to take his order one rainy morning. "I'll bet you didn't get them from a beauty parlor."

It had seemed such an innocuous remark, nothing like the heavy-handed approach she'd grown used to hearing from the truckers who frequented the café. Victoria had smiled and said no, she hadn't, and would he like toast or muffins with his eggs?

He'd chatted pleasantly as she served his meal and that night, when her shift ended, he'd been waiting outside the café.

"How about getting some supper?" he'd asked, and when she'd turned him down he'd said well, would she like a lift home, instead?

She'd said no to that, too. But the streets were deserted and the wind was frigid, and when he'd asked her if she really preferred freezing to death or riding in comfort, she'd laughed and given in. Craig had taken her to the door and waited until she was safely inside, and then driven off, leaving Victoria more impressed by his good manners than by his flashy car.

He'd turned up at the café a lot after that, drawing oohs and aahs from the other waitresses with his good looks and free spending. But Victoria hadn't much cared about any of that. She'd been taken by other things: his apparent sincerity, his decency and, most of all, his touching concern for her welfare.

"Let me make you feel better, baby," he'd say in a soothing voice.

Victoria picked up the brush and drew it slowly through her hair as she remembered. There'd never been any sexual meaning to it; Craig would massage her shoulders at the end of a particularly tiring day, or take her out to dinner when she thought she'd sooner die than serve one more hamburger. And she had let him. No one, not in all her nineteen years, had ever worried much about how she felt. She had never known her father, and her mother had always been busy trying to make ends meet. Being cared for was a new and wonderful experience.

Not that she'd let Craig indulge her with material things. She hadn't needed "things," she'd needed affection, and Craig, damn him, had known it. She'd been almost pathetically grateful for each kind word, each gentle kiss on the cheek. As her mother's illness had worsened, she'd turned to him more and more for comfort.

"Let me make you feel better, baby," he'd say, putting his arms around her.

Victoria's mouth tightened. What a fool she'd been! His caresses had grown more lingering, his touch more personal, but she hadn't read the signs at all, not until that last terrible night when he'd suddenly pressed her down into the Cadillac's soft leather seats.

"Let me make you feel better, baby," he'd said thickly, and the soft words had suddenly taken on a dark and ominous meaning.

When she'd felt his hands moving on her, she'd pleaded with him to stop. Then she'd threatened. Finally, she'd struggled in blind panic. But, in the end, Craig had done what he'd wanted.

He'd seemed genuinely amazed that she wouldn't see him after that night, but he'd got over his surprise quickly enough; less than a month later, the local paper had announced his forthcoming wedding to a girl from Chicago. They'd been engaged for several months, the article said, and you could read between the lines and see that her family had even more money than his.

Victoria's hands trembled as she put down the hairbrush. She could still remember what came next in detail. The shock of learning she was pregnant, and with it the bone-chilling realization that her mother might not survive knowing that her daughter had somehow repeated her own terrible mistake. And mixed in with all of it was the determination that her child was entitled to a far better life than she could possibly give it.

Dr. Ronald had proposed two solutions. Abortion or adoption, he'd said, and there hadn't been anything to think about, really; she'd known that she couldn't bring herself to end the pregnancy.

"Don't worry, Victoria," he'd said when she'd told him. "I'll handle everything."

And he had. Her pregnancy hadn't shown beneath the oversize sweaters and loose clothing that was all the rage that year. He had made all of the arrangements for the hospital in Chicago, where she'd given birth to a daughter at seven-thirty in the evening on a frigid sixteenth day of January, and then he'd picked her up and driven her back to Broadwell himself, so that three days later she was at her mother's bedside, answering questions about the "flu" that had kept her away while the doctor smiled his reassurance across the tubes that snaked in and out of her mother's body.

"You did the right thing, Victoria," he'd said later.

Victoria blinked back her tears as she remembered. She *had* done the right thing, she knew it in her heart. It was just that no one had ever told her how badly she'd ache for the child she'd never seen. Sometimes, seeing Susu's sweet face, the pain was almost more than she could bear. How could Alexandra Campbell have turned her back on all this? She had had it all; a child to love and Roarke—Roarke, who was everything any woman could ever want; Roarke, who was—who was——

She lifted her chin and met her own eyes in the mirror. There was only one way out, and she'd known it for days. She had to leave the island before things went any further, before——

"Toria?"

Roarke's voice, and his light rap at the door, startled her. Her gaze flew to the clock. He was earlier than usual, the earliest he'd been in days.

"Toria? Are you in there?"

She drew a steadying breath, then got to her feet. "Yes," she called. "Just a second."

By the time she flung open the door, she had a smile pasted to her lips. But it wasn't good enough to fool him; she could see that in the way that he frowned when he saw her.

"You missed Susanna," she said brightly. "I didn't realize you'd be home this early. You should have phoned—I'd have kept her up late."

"I came to see you." His voice was sharp, almost curt. "We have to talk."

Victoria bit down on her bottom lip. "Yes," she said after a few seconds. "You're right. We do."

Roarke nodded grimly as he closed the door behind him. "Good. I'm glad you agree."

"Actually—actually, I was going to—to talk to you after dinner." She turned away. "Roarke, I've been thinking. I—I can't stay on here any longer."

"Yes." He puffed out his breath. "I thought it was something like that."

"I wish I could explain why I have to leave," she said softly. "But I can't."

He laughed harshly. "Hell, what's there to explain?" He brushed past her and walked to the french windows. "You're unhappy here. I've known that for days."

"No. No, it isn't that."

Roarke swung toward her, and her heart clenched when she saw the undisguised pain in his eyes.

"Don't lie to me, damn it! Even a fool could tell you're not happy."

Let him believe what he wants, Victoria told herself. What does it matter, as long as you get off this island? But then she looked into his eyes again, and she knew that she couldn't let it happen this way. She had lied to him about too many things; she could not lie about this.

"It has nothing to do with being here," she said softly.

But Roarke wasn't listening. "Is it Susu?" he demanded.

Victoria stared at him. "Susu? No, of course not. I love Susu——"

"It's the island, then. There's not a hell of a lot to do here, especially at night."

She smiled. "Are you complaining because I've beaten you at Scrabble three times running?"

"Twice," he said quickly, and smiled, but then his brows drew together in a dark furrow. "If you like, I'll have the helicopter fly you to San Juan for a couple of days, or to Ponce——"

"No. I mean, that's very kind, but I don't much care if I never see a city again." Victoria hesitated. "If—if I seem unhappy," she said finally, "it has nothing to do with the island, or with Susu——"

"Or with me?"

Her eyes flew to his. He was watching her with an intensity that was almost like a caress. Lie to him, she thought again, tell him whatever you must...

"Is it me, Toria?" He took a step toward her. "Jesus, is it being with me that's making your eyes so dark with sorrow?"

A lump rose in her throat, and she knew that she could not have told him anything but the truth at that moment if her life had depended on it.

"Oh, no," she whispered. "No, it's not you, Roarke. Never you."

He looked at her for what seemed a long time, and then he cleared his throat.

"What is it, then?"

"I just—I have to leave the island. I'll stay until you find someone to——"

"What you need is a night out," he said briskly, his voice cutting across hers.

Victoria stared at him. After all this, that he'd offer such a simple suggestion seemed almost unbelievable.

"A night out? You mean, in San Juan? But I just told you, I——"

"There's a voodoo ceremony tonight, when the moon touches the horizon."

Her eyes widened. "Voodoo?"

"You have half an hour to get ready."

"No. I mean, I can't. I'm leaving——"

"No, you're not."

"But——"

He stepped closer to her and cupped her face in his hands. It was the first time he had touched her since that night in the garden, and the feel of his hands on her seemed to send a lightning bolt sizzling between them.

Roarke had felt it, too; she could tell by the way he looked at her.

"Do you really want to leave me?" he asked softly.

"I must."

Her whispered answer was muffled against his mouth. His kiss was gentle at first, and then he groaned and pulled her into his arms. His mouth opened on hers, and she felt the swift, sweet thrust of his tongue.

It was he who drew back. When she opened her eyes, she found him watching her through pupils so dark and enormous that she felt, for one dizzying instant, that she might fall into his eyes and drown.

"Tell me you still want to leave," he said, "and I'll phone for the helicopter right now."

She wanted to. But how could she tell him anything, when he was looking at her like that? A triumphant smile curved across his mouth.

"No," he said, tracing his fingertips along her hot cheek to the pulse leaping in the hollow of her throat, "I didn't think so."

By the time she trusted herself to speak, he was gone.

The moon seemed tinged with blood as it touched the black sea. Orange flames from a fire licked hungrily into the night, casting eerie shadows across the men and women gathered on the sandy plateau.

Victoria shivered a little and edged closer into the protective circle of Roarke's arm.

"Do they know we're here?" she whispered.

Roarke smiled. "Yes, of course. We were invited."

"What's that?" She nodded toward a flat boulder on which were set candles, flowers, and objects which she couldn't quite identify.

"An altar." He bent his head so that his lips were close to her ear. "Those are things sacred to the *Loa* they're honoring tonight."

She glanced up at him. *"Loa?"*

"It means '"god."'" There's a pantheon of gods in voodoo—nature gods, both good and evil."

Victoria shuddered again. "There aren't going to be any sacrifices or anything, are there?"

Roarke shook his head. "No," he said firmly. "Not on this island."

"What will they do, then?"

"Dance. That's what tonight's gathering is all about. See? There's the *hungan*—the priest. He's going to make an offering to the *Loa*."

"You said there wouldn't be any sacrifices."

He chuckled. "This one won't hurt anybody." The *hungan* bent over the fire and tipped something into it; a bright blue flame shot into the sky and then died. "Rum," Roarke whispered. "For the god Legba. Now the priest will bless the drums. They're just near the altar. See?"

Victoria nodded. She watched as the *hungan* struck each drum lightly, then sprinkled it with rum. Men stepped out of the shadows, lifted the instruments, then fell in a straggly line behind the priest and walked three times around the altar.

"What are they doing now?"

"Blessing the drums, I think." Roarke nodded. "Yes, here we go. The women are stepping into the firelight, and now the men."

The drummers settled down on the sand, just beyond the fire. A slow, throbbing beat rose into the night, and slowly the worshipers began to dance. The steps of each dancer were different; Roarke explained that the dancers were honoring the gods Damballa and Erzilie. The beat of the drums grew louder and faster, and the motions of the dancers became more agitated as they moved around the fire.

Suddenly, a woman threw back her head. Her features became contorted, she cried out as if she were in pain, and she fell to the sand, her body twisting in a frenzy.

Victoria dug her fingers into Roarke's arm. "What's happened to her?"

"She's been taken over by a spirit."

"Should we help her?"

Roarke laughed softly and drew Victoria back into the shadows. "No. It's all right, Toria. That's just what she wanted to happen."

Victoria gave a shaky laugh. "She wanted to scream like that and writhe on the ground?"

"She wants to be cleansed." Roarke put his hand on her shoulder and turned her toward him. "Or to offer her thanks, or pray for good luck, or any one of a dozen things." In the bright glow of the moonlight, Victoria could see the sudden tightening of his mouth. "She wants to change what has been, Toria, and guarantee what is to come. Does anyone want less?"

Victoria drew in her breath. "No," she said in a low voice. "No one does. But it's not like that in the real world. You can't undo what's happened any more than you can read the future."

Roarke's hands slid to her waist. "You can set the past aside."

"That's not true." Her voice was swift, almost slurred. "What's done is done, it's part of your life."

"Then you can make peace with it."

Victoria looked into his face. "Can you?"

"Yes, if you can find the way."

Was he talking about his failed marriage? she wondered suddenly. She wanted to ask him, to know once and for all if his former wife still mattered to him, but what right had she to ask Roarke about his past when she could not—dared not—speak of her own?

A tremor went through her, and he drew her close into his arms.

"Toria? Are you cold?"

She shook her head. "No," she whispered. "I was just—I was thinking that the people gathered around that fire are asking their gods for a lot."

Roarke nodded. "For miracles," he said softly. His hands slipped to her chin and he tilted her face to his. "But then, that's what a night like this is all about, Toria. It's a night to ask for miracles."

He bent to her slowly, his eyes holding hers. "Toria." He whispered her name as he gathered her to him, whispered it again, and suddenly his mouth was on hers.

For one brief flash, she thought of that night with Craig, and her body tensed. But then Roarke caressed her and she knew that with that one, simple motion he had wiped away all the fear Craig had left behind.

She moaned softly and put her arms around his neck. Her head fell back, baring the long curve of her throat to his lips and teeth.

"Kiss me," he said thickly, and when she raised her face blindly to him, he crushed her mouth beneath his.

His tongue swept along the curve of her lips and she whispered her surrender again as she opened to him. His tongue thrust into her mouth and the taste of him filled her. Her breath quickened; her bones turned fluid and he groaned and ran his hands down her spine to her hips, then cupped her buttocks and brought her against the hardness of his body.

"Roarke," she whispered, and he heard her capitulation in the single word. He swept her up into his arms and stepped further back into the darkness until they were lost in the trees, and then he lay her down on the soft ground and bent over her.

Her dress fell open under his swift fingers. "I can feel the race of your heart, love," he said, cupping his hand over her breast.

It was true; her heart was galloping madly, like a wild thing racing to be set free. Victoria stared up into the darkness, seeing only the gleam of Roarke's eyes, the pale silhouette of his face above her. In the distance, the beat of the drums had reached a demonic intensity. A voice cried out again. It was a night for miracles, Roarke had said—but morning would come soon enough, and there were precious few miracles that could stand up to the harsh blaze of the sun.

Suddenly, what was about to happen seemed impossible. She had to leave this place, she *had* to. But if she did this—if she let Roarke make love to her—how could she ever get away?

"No," she said, and she pushed her hands against his chest.

"Toria? What is it?"

She turned her face to the side, praying that it was too dark for him to see the tears rising in her eyes.

"I—I can't do this," she said in a broken whisper.

She heard the harsh exhalation of his breath. There was a long silence, and then he gathered her in his arms and drew her up beside him.

"Forgive me," he said. "This is the wrong place, the wrong time..."

Victoria nodded. "Yes," she whispered, "it is."

It was easier to tell him that than to tell him the truth, she thought, as he put his arm around her waist and they began the slow walk back to the house. There would never be a right time and place. Not for them.

CHAPTER EIGHT

SHE was in love with him. Why had it taken her until tonight to realize it? Victoria tossed in her bed as the dark hours whispered past, trying to understand what had happened, to somehow go back and rip the moment from the fabric of time.

The beat of the voodoo drums slackened, until finally it mirrored the slow, sad beat of her heart. Roarke, she thought, Roarke, and the tears she'd worked so hard to suppress rose in her eyes and slid down her cheeks. Now, more than ever before, she knew she had to leave the island. Coming here had been wrong, staying on had been worse, and now she had to put an end to it.

Somewhere in the darkness a night bird cried out, its voice as lonely and anguished as her heart. Victoria rolled over and buried her face in the pillow. There was only one way to get away from here, and that was to do it quickly and cleanly, without confronting Roarke. Whatever he thought of her, when he found her gone it would be better than what he'd think of her if he ever learned the truth.

Roarke always left for his office by eight o'clock. What she'd do, then, was wait in her room until she knew he was gone, then pack and go downstairs. If someone— Roarke's pilot, or one of the local fishermen—was willing to help her, fine. If not, there were charter services that would come and pick her up, and to hell with the cost.

Victoria closed her eyes wearily as dawn tinted the sky pink. The cost of staying in this place even a day longer was one she could no longer afford.

At a few minutes before eight in the morning, she heard the whirr of the engine as the 'copter rose over the roof. Roarke was gone, then. Her throat tightened, but she rose quickly and dressed in her white linen traveling suit, then tossed the rest of her clothing into her suitcase. The hard part lay ahead: she'd have to say goodbye to Constancia, and to Susu. She wouldn't think about that. No. She'd just do what had to be done.

One of the maids had got Susanna up. She was eating her oatmeal in the kitchen with Constancia, and she smiled and held out her arms as Victoria came into the room.

"Mòrning, Toria," she sang out happily.

Victoria ached to pick her up but she didn't dare, for fear that holding the little girl in her arms might prove her undoing.

"Hello, Susu," she said softly.

"*Buenos días, señorita*. It is a lovely..." Constancia's words drifted to silence as she looked at Victoria. The housekeeper's dark eyes took in her sensible pumps, her stockings, her suit and silk blouse, then narrowed as they fixed on her face. "You are going somewhere?" she asked slowly.

"Yes," Victoria said briskly. "I am. Constancia——" Suddenly, to her horror, her voice quavered, then broke. She stared at the older woman, then turned quickly away. "Please," she whispered, "would you—would you just see to it that Susanna finishes her breakfast?"

"*Señorita*, what is it?"

"Nothing. I just—I'll be back in a minute, Constancia."

"*Por favor*, Señorita Hamilton..."

Victoria waved her hand in front of her face as she brushed past the surprised woman.

"I'm all right," she said. "I just—I just need a minute——"

She stumbled into the hall and then to the library, tears streaming down her cheeks. She had to do this now, before she lost courage. Going down to the docks, asking around until she found someone willing to take her to San Juan, might take half the morning, and by then she'd be lucky if she could still think.

She wiped the backs of her hands across her eyes, then reached for the telephone on the desk. Her fingers shook as she punched the buttons, then waited, head bowed, for the information operator to come on the line.

"Yes," she said, as soon as she heard the polite, impersonal voice. "Yes, please. I'd like the number of a charter helicopter service. No, I don't have a name, operator, I just want someone who'll be willing to pick me up on Isla de la Pantera and take me to——"

"Hang up the phone, Victoria."

She spun around, eyes wide. Roarke was standing in the terrace doorway, watching her.

"Did you hear me? I told you to hang up."

The operator's voice rang tinnily in her ear as she did as he'd ordered. Her heart rose in her throat. God, he was so angry! No, that wasn't really the word to describe it. He'd been angry that day she'd pushed her way into the Campbell building, and angry the evening she'd been the cause of the accident that had all but demolished his car. But he'd never looked quite like this—his face dark and threatening, his eyes cold as stones, sweeping over her now, as Constancia's had, coming to rest finally on her face.

"That's a handsome outfit," he said evenly. A cool smile twisted across his mouth. "Of course, that's not usually the kind of suit you wear when you take Susanna swimming, is it?''

Victoria swallowed hard. "What are you doing here, Roarke?"

His lips drew back from his teeth. "A good question. In fact, it's such a good question that I think I'll ask it first. What are *you* doing here, Victoria?"

"I was—I was——"

He laughed. "You were much more articulate with the telephone operator. You were getting the number of an air taxi, isn't that right?"

She swallowed again. "Roarke——"

He took a step forward, and his wide-shouldered body seemed to fill the doorway.

"How neatly you planned it. A sexy little farewell on the beach last night..."

"That's not true!"

"...followed by a quick getaway this morning." His mouth turned down as he moved toward her. "What a nice surprise for me, when I got home this evening."

Tears rose in her eyes. "It wasn't like that, Roarke. I wanted to tell you—I *tried* to tell you——"

"Were you planning on a note, Victoria?" His face twisted as he seized her by the shoulders. "Or was even that too much to ask for? Were you just going to cut and run..."

"Roarke, please——"

"...without so much as a handshake?"

"I—I was just trying to make it easier for both of us. When I heard the helicopter leave, I thought——" Her head fell forward. "I told you last night—I can't stay here any longer. But you didn't want to listen."

He clasped her face and forced her to look at him. "You're damned right I didn't!"

"I thought I'd just—I'd just go, without any more discussion."

"And what about last night?" A tight smile angled across his face. "Were you pretending, when I took you in my arms?"

Victoria closed her eyes. "Don't, please."

His hands tightened on her. "Answer me."

"You have no right to——"

"Okay, then, I'll just find out for myself."

She cried out as his mouth fastened on hers and she tried desperately to twist free, but his kiss was as hard and uncompromising as the grip of his hands and she gave in to it finally, knowing there was no other way to end this than to submit. Yet it was that very compliance that proved her undoing, for when she stopped struggling against him what was happening between them changed. One hand remained holding her face still for his kiss, but the other slipped to her throat, then to her shoulder, and then his arm swept around her and he gathered her to him.

"Toria," he whispered, his mouth still on hers, and when his lips closed on hers again it was in a kiss that was gentle. He was asking now, not demanding, giving as much as he was taking, and all her determination to resist him fled. She made a whimper of surrender and her body curved toward his until they were straining against each other, heart racing against heart.

They stood that way for a long time, and then Roarke clasped her arms and put her from him. He looked at her flushed face, at the rapid rise and fall of her breasts, and a quick, triumphant smile curved over his mouth.

"You're not going anywhere."

It took all her concentration to speak calmly. "Nothing's changed, Roarke. I'm leaving."

"No, you are not. What you're going to do is go to your room and change your clothes."

"Just because you kissed me——"

"We're taking the boat out." He glanced at his watch. "I'll give you five minutes to change, unless you want to spend a day on the water dressed like that."

She stared at him. "You really didn't hear anything I said, did you?"

"I heard it." His voice was smug. "And I proved how meaningless it was."

Victoria felt a quick flutter of anger. "That may have worked with your wife, Roarke, but——"

His eyes flashed a warning. "Don't speak of things you know nothing about."

"I do know. Constancia told me that there's still something between you. And if—if this is the way you dealt with your wife..."

"Two minutes," he said grimly as he glanced at his watch again. "And then we'll board the boat with you dressed just as you are."

"Damn you, Roarke, are you deaf? I am leaving this island, and I'm leaving right now."

"Really?" He put his hands on his hips. "And just how do you propose to do that?"

"I'm perfectly capable of chartering a——"

He laughed. "A helicopter? Only if you have three hundred bucks."

"A boat, then. Surely there are boats that——"

"Probably. But I don't know where you'll find someone willing to come all the way out here to collect you."

Victoria gritted her teeth. "I'll find another way."

"There is no other way." His brows rose as he correctly read the expression on her face. "If you're thinking of asking somebody on Isla de la Pantera to take you to San Juan, or even to Ponce, you can forget about it. There's not a man on this island who'd do it without my say-so."

She stared at him in amazement. How could she have forgotten this side of him, especially since she had seen it all before? That imperious lift of his chin, the arrogant smile that said he owned the world—he was Roarke Campbell, that was the message. And no one defied him, especially not in his private little kingdom.

"You are so damned sure of yourself," she said tightly.

He laughed. "Yes. I am."

"My God," she said softly, "that's what this is all about, isn't it? You're the king of the hill, and I've had the temerity to try and challenge you."

Roarke folded his arms across his chest. "Think what you like. All I'm telling you is that you will not leave this island without my permission."

She gave a toss of her head. "Goodbye, Roarke."

"Victoria."

She heard the soft warning in his voice, saw it in his eyes, and a little warning flash went through her. But it was too late to back off, she'd made her decision and there was nothing left to do but exit as quickly as possible. She swung on her heel, back and shoulders ramrod straight, and marched toward the door.

"Victoria!" His voice roared after her, and her heart beat a sudden tattoo. He was all bluff, she told herself. After all, what could he do to stop her?

The answer came just as she reached out for the doorknob. Roarke's hands came down on her shoulders. She cried out as he spun her to him, and then there was time for one quick glimpse of his face, tight and dark with anger, before he lifted her into his arms and strode rapidly through the open french windows to the terrace beyond.

"Roarke, are you crazy?" Victoria beat her hands against his shoulders, but it was useless. He just kept walking steadily across the grass, around the side of the house and to the driveway where his Jeep stood parked in the shade of a palm tree. He dumped her into it without ceremony, then climbed into the driver's seat.

"Buckle your seat belt," he said as he slammed on the ignition.

"We've played this scene before, remember?" She was trembling, with rage more than fear. "I'm not impressed."

"I don't do things to impress people, Victoria." He reached past her and closed her belt, his hands brushing lightly over her breasts. "I thought you'd learned at least that much about me by now."

The Jeep shot forward, its tires flinging gravel from the road as he jammed his foot down on the accelerator.

"For God's sake—why are you doing this?"

He stepped down on the brakes and brought the Jeep to a screeching halt, then laid his hands flat on the steering wheel while he stared straight ahead. He was fighting for composure, she thought suddenly, and the realization was almost as amazing as what happened next.

Roarke took a deep breath and turned to her. "Yes," he said. "I suppose I should have told you that first. I'm doing it because I don't want you to leave the island."

Victoria's mouth turned down. "That's not exactly news."

He gave her a smile so swift and strange that she wasn't really sure it had been a smile at all.

"And because I've fallen in love with you," he said, and before she could make up her mind that she hadn't hallucinated those softly spoken words, he turned away, shifted into gear, and sent the Jeep careering down the narrow road that led to the docks.

Neither of them said anything more until they were on board the cruiser and headed out to sea. What could you say, Victoria kept thinking, when the man you'd fallen in love with told you that he loved you, too? It had been easy to be angered by his behavior when she'd thought he was playing at being God, but hearing him say he loved her, having him look at her the way he had, with all the vulnerability in the world suddenly glittering in his eyes, had undone her.

But as the land fell further and further away, she began to think straight again. Roarke's admission changed nothing; she still had to leave. In fact, now it was more imperative than ever.

"Toria?"

She looked up. He was standing at the wheel, watching her. But he'd put on dark smoked glasses; she couldn't see his eyes, and somehow that was disconcerting.

"There's some clothing in the locker below—cutoff denims of mine and some T-shirts." He smiled. "Nothing will fit very well, but you might be more comfortable out of that suit."

She wet her lips with the tip of her tongue. "I think we should go back," she said quietly.

Roarke shook his head. "Not until we've talked."

"Roarke——"

"That's why I brought us out here. It's quiet, and there's no one to interrupt us." He nodded toward a dark smudge on the horizon. "There's a key just ahead. It's uninhabited, and few people visit. Go on and get into something cooler. By the time you're changed, we'll be anchored."

She opened her mouth to argue, but what was the sense? She was on his boat, in the middle of the sea. He would take her back to shore when he was ready and not a moment sooner, and they both knew it. Sighing, Victoria got to her feet and made her way to the cabin.

She did the best she could with the clothing she found, but she felt foolish when she came back on deck. His shorts fitted well enough through the hips but they gapped at the waist, and the smallest shirt she'd found hung almost to her knees. She hadn't bothered about shoes; her feet were bare. In fact, all she had on besides the shorts and shirt were her panties—she'd worn a lace teddy under her suit, which she couldn't very well wear under the shorts.

She came on deck and paused in the cabin doorway. They were lying at anchor in a tiny cove, surrounded on three sides by dark green, palm-fringed rocky shores. Roarke smiled when he looked up and saw her, and she laughed self-consciously as she thrust her fingers into her wind-tossed hair and pushed it back from her face.

"Well, you were right about this outfit being more comfortable," she said, "although I don't think it's going to win any fashion awards."

"You look lovely, and dressed just right for Dolphin Key."

He was dressed just right, too, she thought. While she'd been gone, he'd stripped down to shorts as old and disreputable as hers, and he'd taken off his shirt. His body was sun-gold and hard-muscled, beautiful in its male symmetry. There was a little rivulet of sweat beading down from the hollow of his throat to the dark, silken hair that whorled across his chest, and suddenly she ached to go into his arms and put her mouth to his throat, to taste the heat of his skin and the salt of his sweat . . .

"What is it, Toria?"

She shook her head. "Nothing. I just—I wish you'd take us back," she said, looking away from him.

He came toward her slowly, stopping when he was a touch away. She could feel the heat coming off his body.

"Toria." He touched her hair, and she turned to him reluctantly. He had taken off his sunglasses; she could see the darkness in his eyes and it made her breath catch. "Why have you never asked me about Alexandra?"

She swallowed dryly. "Who?"

"My wife." His mouth twisted. "My *ex*-wife. You've asked Constancia about her, but not me."

"I—I just felt it was none of my business."

"And yet you think you know about her—and about our relationship."

She was puzzled, at first, and then she remembered what she'd said to him a little while ago. Color flared in her cheeks.

"I had no right to say that," she said quickly. "I mean, I suppose I understand how sex can be a force between two people."

Roarke touched her hair again, this time running his fingers through the tangled silken skein.

"Can you?" His voice was a little rough. He smiled. "Funny. I'd have thought you didn't know very much about passion."

"I don't." She touched her tongue to her lips. "I mean, I've never felt—I never really wanted——" She let out her breath. "There's a lot you don't know about me," she said helplessly.

His hands went to her shoulders. "I want to learn."

"Roarke," Her heart fluttered in her breast. If he kept holding her, standing so close to her, she would be lost. "Roarke, please. I—I'm flattered by what you said, but——"

He laughed huskily. "I don't want you to feel flattered," he said, bending toward her and touching his mouth to her temple. "I want you to tell me you've fallen in love with me, too."

Her eyes closed as he kissed her cheek. "Don't do that."

"Why? Don't you like it when I touch you, Toria?"

She shuddered as he moved his hand to her throat. His fingers drifted over her skin, then lay lightly over the throbbing beat of her pulse.

"Roarke——"

Oh, God, was that croaking whisper hers? He had no right to do this to her, damn him. They were going to talk, that was what he'd said, that was why he'd brought her out here.

She cried out as his hand slipped under her T-shirt and moved against her skin.

"No," she said. "Please, don't. You said—you said you wanted to talk to me."

"I am talking," he said gruffly. He pushed the hair back from her neck and kissed the exposed skin, then breathed lightly into her ear. "Just listen, and you'll hear every word."

"Roarke." Victoria reached out to push him away. But his skin was so hot, satin-smooth over his taut muscles, so silky where the dark hair lay curled on his chest. Touching him sent a tingle through her fingertips, and somehow, instead of putting him from her, she found herself exploring the curve of his shoulder, the line of his collarbone. "Roarke," she said again, but this time the word was a sigh.

"Yes, love," he whispered. "That's right. Touch me, while I——" He caught his breath as his hand slipped to her breast. "Ah, Victoria. Your skin is as hot as the sun. You feel so——"

"No. No, don't."

She moaned softly as he cupped her naked breasts in his hands. His thumbs moved across the nipples and she arched toward him, eyes closed in ecstasy.

"God," he groaned. "Toria. Let me—let me——"

Let him? She could no more have stopped him than she could have stopped the waves of the ocean. This was what she had wanted for days, for weeks, from the moment she had first seen him. Her arms lifted to him as he drew off her T-shirt. She heard the quick intake of his breath as he looked at her, and then he drew her fiercely into his arms so that her breasts were pressed tightly against his chest.

"I knew you would feel this way," he whispered. "So soft. So warm." He drew back and cupped her face. "Look at me," he said. Her breath caught when she did; his face was taut with desire, his eyes black with need. "Tell me you want me."

"Yes," she said unashamedly. "Oh, yes. I want you."

Triumph glittered in his eyes. "And do you love me, Toria?"

Lie to him, she thought, lie to him now as you've lied to him about everything else. But how could she, when he was kissing her as he was? How could she, when his mouth was at her breast, his teeth and lips tugging lightly at her flesh? How could she, when her heart and soul were so clearly his for the taking?

He lifted her face to his and looked deep into her eyes. "Tell me," he said fiercely.

The words burst from her throat. "I love you," she said, and when she saw how her admission transformed him she felt a swift surge of joy unlike any she'd ever known before. "Oh, Roarke, I love you."

He lifted her in his arms, holding her tightly to him, and he kissed her and kissed her until she felt as if she and he were at the core of a spinning universe.

"Toria," he whispered, and he drew her slowly down onto the warm teak deck.

The sun blazed down as he stripped away her clothing, and its heat paled beside the heat in Roarke's eyes as he looked at her lying before him. She felt molten, as if the passion in him had turned her liquid. But when he rose to his feet and opened the snap on his cutoffs, a roiling wave of panic rose in her stomach.

"Don't," she said in a breathless whisper.

Roarke paused, his eyes darkening as he looked at her. He dropped to his knees beside her and lifted her to him.

"What is it, Toria?"

She shook her head. How could she tell him that, for one awful moment, she had seen not his face but another man's, that suddenly her body had tightened with fear?

But he knew, somehow. His face contorted, his lips drawing back from his teeth in an animal grimace.

"That's why you passed out on me in the elevator that day, isn't it?" The fury in his voice was all the more terrifying for the cold, precise sound of it. "Who's the son-of-a-bitch who hurt you? I'll kill him! I'll hunt him down and——"

She leaned toward him and buried her face against his sun-warmed skin.

"Please," she whispered. "For both our sakes, take me to San Juan. Let me get on a plane and go back to the States."

His arms went around her, and he crushed her to him, until their heartbeats seemed to be one.

"You don't have to be afraid of me, don't you know that?" He bent his head and pressed his mouth to her hair. "I'd never hurt you."

Tears rolled down her cheeks. "It's not that, Roarke. It's—it's—there's so much about me you—you don't know."

He smiled into her eyes and he put her gently from him. "Yes," he said softly. "I want to learn, Toria." Once again he bent to her and kissed her mouth. "I want to learn what you taste like." She caught her breath as his hand swept lightly over her naked breast. "And what you feel like."

"Roarke——"

"I want to see your eyes darken as you lie beneath me." His voice thickened as he eased her down onto the deck. "To hear you cry out my name as I move inside you."

His head and shoulders blotted out the sun as he kissed her—sweet, teasing kisses that drove the fear from her heart. She gasped as his hand moved over her, stroking her flesh until it bloomed with desire, and she moaned softly against his mouth. Her arms lifted and wound around his neck, her lips parted, and she began kissing him, too, each kiss wilder and deeper than the last, until nothing mattered but Roarke and this moment.

Her throat tightened when he drew back again and opened his cutoffs. But she made herself watch him, and when she saw his naked body she knew that its power was matched by its beauty, and that there was nothing to fear. He came down to her again; she sighed as he kissed her mouth and throat, her breasts and belly, and it was only when he slipped his hands under her and lifted her hips to him that she felt a flutter of panic.

"No," she whispered, but his fingers were moving, stroking lightly between her thighs where her flesh was moist with wanting him.

"I want to taste you," he said thickly, "to imprint your scent and your heat on my soul."

She cried out as he put his mouth on her. A kaleidoscope of colors danced inside her closed eyelids, and she lifted her arms to him and called his name.

Roarke made a growling sound of triumph. "Yes," he said, and he knelt between her legs and, with one swift, deep thrust, sheathed himself in her body.

Victoria felt herself shatter like a crystal, burst into a million shards of spinning glass, and then Roarke exploded within her. She cried out and clasped his head, bringing him down to her so that she could kiss him, and then, finally, he collapsed against her.

"I'm sorry, love," he said. "God, I wanted our first time to be perfect."

"It was perfect," she whispered against his shoulder.

"It was over too soon." He kissed her throat. "Hell, I was no better than a schoolboy. But I've wanted you so badly for so long..."

His words brought back reality. A tremor went through her, and he rose up on his elbows and looked down at her.

"Toria? What is it?"

"Nothing," she said. Tears rose in her eyes, and she turned her face away.

"Darling, tell me. Please, what's wrong?"

She drew a shuddering breath and shook her head. What could she tell him? Dear Lord, what could she *ever* tell him?

Roarke took her face in his hand and gently turned it to him. "Did I hurt you?"

"No. Oh, no, you didn't hurt me." She smiled and blinked back her tears. "You were wonderful."

He smiled too. "What every man wants to hear."

Her answering smile trembled, then vanished. "It's just that—that nothing's changed, you see. I'm still— I'm still the same Victoria——" She broke off in horror. Victoria Winters, she'd almost said, but she couldn't do that. Even the name he knew her by was a lie.

Roarke kissed her. "And a good thing too," he said gently. "A man doesn't want to tumble head over heels for a woman and have her change into someone else before his very eyes." He smiled. "But I'd love you, even if you did."

Victoria closed her eyes. "Roarke——"

"Now, what are these deep, dark secrets I don't know about you?" He laughed softly and rolled onto his side, taking her with him. "Will you sneak bonbons into our bed and drop cake crumbs on the pillows?"

Our bed, she thought, our bed.

"Or is there a warrant out for your arrest?" Her eyes flew open and he laughed again. "You're an ax murderer. No? A bank robber?" He tweaked her nose. "Well, then, the library police are after you for overdue books."

Despite herself, she smiled. "Has anyone ever told you that you're a crazy man?"

His grin faded. "The only thing I want to hear you tell me," he said huskily, "is that you love me."

Victoria's smile trembled. "You know I do."

Roarke drew her to him and kissed her, over and over, each kiss sweeter than the last, until she felt as if she were close to drowning in a sea of pleasure.

"That's all I need to know," he whispered, enfolding her in his arms. "Nothing else means a damn. Remember what I told you last night? What's past is history, love. It's what waits ahead that matters."

It sounded so simple. Victoria wanted to believe it with all her heart, even though her brain was reminding her, in a cold little voice, that it could not possibly be true.

But what did that cool voice of warning have to do with the man holding her in his arms? What did it have to do with the way he was kissing her and touching her, with the feel of his body moving against hers or the salt taste of his skin?

And, when he finally entered her again, the voice faded to a whisper, then died in the swift, rushing pound of her blood.

"I love you," Roarke whispered, and, for just a little while that was the only truth on their piece of the restless sea.

CHAPTER NINE

THE sun was low in the sky by the time they weighed anchor and began motoring back to Isla de la Pantera. Roarke stood at the wheel with Victoria in front of him, his arm around her waist. They had spent the long day in each other's arms, making love to each other and drowsing, padding to the cabin in the late afternoon to share a makeshift meal of crackers, cheese, and white wine. It had been the most glorious day of Victoria's life—and now it was coming to an end.

She shivered, and Roarke drew her back against him. "Are you cool, sweetheart?"

"No. I'm fine."

He nuzzled her hair away from her ear, then bent and kissed her throat.

"This has been the happiest day of my life," he said softly.

Victoria sighed, "I was thinking that, too."

But even as she said it, her throat closed with emotion. It would have been better to have slipped away this morning, as she'd planned. She was still a woman trapped in the worst kind of lie—only now, she'd let an already impossible situation become even more twisted. How could she leave Roarke now? And yet—how could she stay with him?

"Toria?" Roarke's arms tightened around her. "I've been thinking. I don't want to go back to the real world just yet."

Victoria laid her head back against him and sighed deeply. "I know. It would be so much easier to just stay out here forever."

Suddenly, he drew back on the throttle. The roar of the engines dropped to a whisper as Roarke turned her in his arms and smiled at her.

"I have an idea," he said softly.

"An idea? What do you mean?"

"Did you get to see much of Puerto Rico before you came to Isla de la Pantera?"

Victoria looked down. "No," she said evasively. "Not much."

"That's what I thought," he said, taking her face in his hands. "But you should, you know." He smiled at her. "The island's beautiful, and filled with contrasts. There are rainforests and caves and beaches as beautiful as any on Isla de la Pantera."

She smiled. "Does the tourist office pay you to make this speech to everybody, *señor*?"

He laughed as he traced the bones of her cheeks with his thumbs. "I'll bet you didn't even get to see very much of San Juan, Condado, and La Fortaleza, or even the old part of the city."

"I—I didn't get to do much sight-seeing, no."

Roarke nodded. "Well, then, that settles it. When we get back to the house I'll phone my office and tell them they can just damn well plan on doing without me for a week or so." He grinned at the puzzled look on her face. "I think we'll go to Ponce first. You can do some shopping there—nothing fancy, though. We'll leave that for San Juan. And then we'll drive north, to——"

"Roarke. What are you talking about?"

The laughter fled from his eyes. "I'm talking about spending the next days and nights alone with you," he said huskily, "without telephones ringing or servants lurking about." He drew her close and kissed her with a slow thoroughness that left her breathless. "I'm talking about making love to you beside a waterfall, about showing you off at the Chart House for dinner."

Her yearning to let it all happen, and her anguish at believing it impossible, must have shown on her face. Roarke drew a rasping breath, and his hands clasped her tightly.

"When I see that look in your eyes," he said tautly, "I know that I want to search out the son-of-a-bitch who hurt you and kill him with my bare hands."

She stared at him. "What do you mean?"

Roarke's mouth twisted. "I'm not a fool, Toria. I can figure it out for myself. There's something haunting you, and that bastard has something to do with it."

"Oh, Roarke," she said softly, closing her eyes, "you should have let me go away this morning."

"Are you afraid whatever it is might change the way I feel about you?" When she said nothing, he gathered her to him. "Don't be," he whispered. "Nothing could ever do that. You must believe me, Victoria."

And suddenly, suddenly she thought that it might be true. Perhaps she could tell him, some day. Perhaps he'd understand——

"Come away with me, sweetheart," he said. "Let me show you how much I love you."

She looked up to tell him that it was impossible. But when she saw the love in his eyes, how could she give him any answer except yes?

The elegant little boutique was set like a jewel along a stretch of Condado beachfront where jewels of one sort or another were commonplace. But even here, where diamonds glittered and designer clothes fought for display space, this particular window held things that were breathtaking in their beauty—especially the blue and green silk dress that lay draped across a white wicker chair.

Victoria couldn't help but sigh. The dress had thin straps and a full skirt. It looked as if it had been fashioned from the sea, she thought wistfully.

"It's a pretty dress, isn't it?" Roarke said softly, dipping his head toward hers.

She smiled at him. "Yes, it's lovely."

"And made for you."

Victoria laughed and tugged at his hand. "Come on, silly. That dress was made for someone who can afford it."

Roarke's brows lifted. "Well, then——"

It took a second until she understood. When she did, she shook her head vigorously.

"Absolutely not."

One corner of his mouth lifted in a teasing grin. "Absolutely not, the lady says." He took her hand, his fingers lacing through hers, and began tugging her toward the shop door. "You'll have to phone my comptroller and tell him that, Victoria. I'm sure he'll be interested to hear that I can't afford that bit of fluff in the window."

"You know what I mean, Roarke. There's not a way in the world I'd let you buy that dress for me."

Roarke rolled his eyes to the heavens. "You'd think the woman would learn, wouldn't you? We've had this conversation before."

Victoria sighed. He was right, they had—in Ponce, where all her protests hadn't kept him from buying her enough silky cotton dresses, shorts, and matching tops to crowd her suitcase to bursting point.

"It makes me happy," he'd kept saying, and she'd been helpless in the face of such irrefutable and loving logic.

But today, here in San Juan, she'd drawn a firm line. The shops along Ashford Avenue glittered with expensive things—earrings and necklaces and pins, crystal flaçons of perfume, clothing bearing labels she'd read about but never actually seen—and Roarke had been eager to buy them all.

"That would be lovely on you," he kept saying, just as he was now, but Victoria had been unmoved.

"No," she said, as she had been saying all day. But this time Roarke ignored her; he merely shrugged his shoulders, stepped past her, and opened the door to the little shop. A saleswoman stepped forward, smiling pleasantly.

"Roarke." Victoria looked at him. "I am not going inside that place."

He folded his arms and leaned back against the open door. "Fine," he said calmly. "I'll just stand here, then." A wicked grin curved across his mouth. "It's another few hours until our dinner reservation. I'm sure the salespeople won't mind."

"Roarke. This is silly..."

He leaned close to her and gave her a smug smile. "Yes. It is. Now, why don't you behave yourself and try that dress on?"

Victoria stared at him, then lifted her chin and flounced past him into the shop.

"Fine," she said coolly. "I'll try it on and then you can explain to the saleswoman that I'm not the least bit interested in buying it. Will that satisfy you?"

She should have known it wouldn't be that simple. Roarke spoke to the clerk in rapid Spanish, there were a lot of *sí, señors* and smiles, and then Victoria found herself in an elegant fitting room, standing before a bank of mirrors, with the saleswoman slipping the blue and green silk dress over her head.

It was even more wonderful than she had imagined, especially with a matching pair of high-heeled sandals and her dark hair drawn back from her temples with a pair of glittering combs.

"The *señorita* looks lovely," the saleswoman said, and Victoria couldn't very well argue, not when even she could see that the blue of the dress matched the blue of her eyes.

"Lovely," Roarke whispered when she stepped into the little salon and pirouetted before him, and when he caught her to him and kissed her, the smiling assistant looked discreetly away.

When she returned to the fitting room to take off the dress and put on her own clothes, she stopped dead. Her own things were gone; in their place was a tumble of silky garments.

"What is all this?" Victoria asked helplessly.

The woman smiled. "Your *novio* asks that you try these things on, *señorita*."

"My what?"

"Your fiancé. He is most charming."

A flush rose in Victoria's cheeks. "Oh, but he's not——" She hesitated. What harm could there be in pretending, just for a little while? It was such a wonderful thing to imagine, a fantasy beyond all fantasies, and it would hurt no one to indulge it for just a little while.

"All right," she said softly. "Let's give him a fashion show, if that's what he wants."

"I think," the assistant said in a conspiratorial whisper, "that he just wishes to make you happy. I have never seen a man smile so when his lady twirls before him in a new dress."

He did look happy, Victoria thought each time she stepped out from behind the curtain. And, by the time she had tried everything on, she was happy, too. There was such joy in pleasing Roarke—for some reason her thoughts darted to the woman he'd once been married to, and she wondered if she had ever got any pleasure at all from making him happy.

When the little fashion show was over, Victoria slipped her own dress on and combed her fingers through her hair. Only the assistant would be disappointed today, she thought suddenly. Well, maybe she'd inquire about a silk scarf or something. It wouldn't make up for the woman's hopes of having made an enormous sale, but——

She caught her breath as she stepped out of the fitting room. Roarke stood waiting at the door, surrounded by stacks of glossy little boxes and sacks.

"Enjoy your new things, *señorita*," the saleswoman said happily, and while Victoria was still trying to come up with a response, Roarke took her by the arm and led her out to a waiting taxi. He handed her inside, then settled next to her with the assorted packages safely in residence on the floor.

Victoria turned toward him, her eyes dark with anger. "What's all this?"

He shrugged. "I couldn't decide which things I liked the best, so I took them all."

Her mouth dropped open. "You took them all? The dresses, the outfits, the gowns——"

He chuckled as he leaned forward and kissed her forehead. "Don't leave out the negligee set. That's my favorite."

Victoria drew a deep breath. "How could you do that to me? I told you I wouldn't let you buy me——"

"Yes. I know." He took her hand and brought it to his lips. "But it gave me more pleasure that I can describe."

"Roarke, that may have worked when we were in Ponce. But——"

"Please, love." His hand tightened on hers. "Please say you'll accept my gift."

Her eyes lifted to his. Please, he'd said, and with that one simple word he'd changed everything. There was something deeply touching in knowing that she held such power over this man who could make the world jump at the snap of his fingers.

Tears rose in her eyes and she ducked her head to hide them. "You're an impossible man," she said briskly.

Roarke laughed softly, put his arm around her, and drew her close to him.

"No," he whispered. "I'm just very much in love."

That night Victoria put on the beautiful new blue and green dress and they dined in a quietly elegant restaurant in Dorado that fronted on the sea. Roarke ordered brandy at the end of their meal and when it arrived he said something in Spanish to the waiter, scrawled his name on their bill, and got to his feet.

"Come on," he said, holding out his hand to Victoria.

Puzzled, she put her hand in his and stood up. "But we haven't had our drinks."

Roarke smiled mysteriously. "Just take your glass with you," he said, and he tucked her free hand into the curve of his arm.

Minutes later they were walking slowly along the darkened beach, Victoria's high-heeled sandals safely tucked into the pockets of Roarke's dinner jacket. He put his arm around her waist and she sighed and leaned her head on his shoulder.

"This is decadent," she said softly. "The smell of the sea, the moonlight on the beach——"

"You mean to tell me they don't do this back home in Broadwell?" Roarke asked innocently.

Victoria smiled. "I don't really think you can compare a movie and a pizza to this."

He laughed. "No brandy, hmm?"

"No brandy, no moonlit Caribbean, no warm sand under your toes——"

"And no me to kiss you," he said huskily. She lifted her face to him and their lips met and clung. After a long while she sighed and put her head on his shoulder again. "So," Roarke said, "tell me what it's like to be a little girl growing up in a small town."

"It's—well, it's a quiet life, I suppose."

He smiled. "Is that the kind of little girl you were? Quiet?"

Victoria sighed. "That's as good a description as any."

"What about brothers or sisters? Didn't you have any?"

She shook her head. "There was just my mother and me." She hesitated. "I had no father," she said slowly. It was the first time in her life she had ever volunteered the information that had always pained her. "None I ever knew, anyway."

Roarke's arm tightened around her. "I'm sorry, sweetheart. That must have been rough."

"It was," she said with simple honesty. "In such a small town, where everyone knows everyone else..." Her voice faded.

"And now your mother is gone?"

"How did you——"

"Well, you said you had no one to go home to."

Victoria nodded. "Yes." She drew a deep breath, then let it out. "She died just over three years ago."

"What happened?" he asked softly.

She sighed. "I guess I'll never really know. She seemed to have a cold, at first, a bad cough. But they did some tests, even tried an operation... She was ill for a long time. At the end, they wanted me to put her into a hospice, but I brought her home. She'd always worked so hard to take care of me——"

Roarke heard the sudden catch in her voice and swung round to face her. "Hey," he whispered, tilting her chin up. "Don't cry, sweetheart. I didn't mean to make you think of sad things."

Victoria shook her head as she sniffed back the tears that had suddenly threatened.

"You didn't. I mean, I was just thinking how happy I've been the last few weeks. Since I—since I met you..."

"Yes," he said softly. "That's how I feel, too." He gave her a long, sweet kiss, and then he smiled and lifted his brandy snifter to hers. "Come on," he said briskly, "drink up. And then we'll go to our suite and sit on the balcony while we count the stars."

Victoria changed from the blue and green dress to the gown and negligee that Roarke had bought her. It was made of ivory silk and lace, and when she saw herself in the bedroom mirror she thought she had never seen anything more lovely.

"It's beautiful," she whispered.

Roarke came up behind her, handsome and powerful in his white dinner jacket and dark pants, and put his hands on her shoulders.

"*You're* beautiful," he said as he kissed her neck. He raised his head and looked at her steadily in the glass. "I love you, Toria. I want you to marry me."

She saw her own eyes grow wide and dark. "Oh, Roarke," she whispered, and for one swift heartbeat she felt a joy so great that it stole her breath away. But then she remembered what she had spent the week trying to forget, and her face paled. "No. I can't. Thank you for asking me, but——"

"Thank you for asking me?" His voice was harsh. "Is that the best you can do?" He spun her toward him, and his eyes fixed on hers. "What is it you're afraid of, Victoria? Why do you keep hiding from me?"

"Hiding? I'm not——"

"It's as if there's a wall between us, and I can't get past it." He drew her to him. "Toria, my love," he said quietly, "don't you believe that I love you?"

She smiled, even though she could feel the sting of tears behind her eyes.

"Yes," she whispered, "I believe it."

Roarke looked at her. "If there's something about yourself you want to tell me," he said steadily, "do it, and know that I'll still love you no matter what it is." He kissed her tenderly. "But if you don't want to say it, whatever it is, that's all right, too. Don't you see? Our lives began the day we met—whatever happened in the past has no meaning."

Her eyes met his. Was it—could it be—true? For the first time, Victoria felt a flutter of hope.

"Do you mean that?"

Roarke put his arm around her shoulders and drew her out to the balcony. "Let me tell you what my life was like before you came along," he said. He drew her down with him onto a padded chaise longue and held her close in his arms. "I got up in the morning, had a few sweet minutes with Susu, then went to my office. At the day's end, I left my office and spent some time with Susu." He smoothed back her hair and dropped a light kiss on her temple. "Except for the time I spent with my daughter, the hours in between were hollow."

Victoria's heart turned over. "My life was like that, too," she whispered. "Only I—I didn't have a child to love."

He nodded. "Susu's made all the difference in my life." He laughed softly. "Sometimes I think how ironic it is that something so wonderful could have come out of a marriage as bad as mine and Alexandra's."

"But I thought—you loved her, didn't you?"

Roarke shook his head. "I suppose I did. Hell, I thought I did. But that was a long time ago."

Victoria sat up and looked at him. "I thought, from what Constancia said, that—that you and she—that there was still something . . ."

He laughed again, but this time the sound was sharp and bitter. "There is," he said. "Susanna."

"You mean—your wife . . ."

"My ex-wife," he said. "Don't ever forget the *ex*."

"She wants custody? Is that what you mean?"

Roarke got to his feet and walked slowly to the railing of the balcony.

"Alexandra never wants the same thing two weeks running," he said, leaning his arms on the rail. "That was one of the things that charmed me, at first, that will-o'-the-wisp quality." He sighed. "But I learned fast that's not what it really is at all, it's just that she's like a greedy child. Something interests her one moment, and the next——" He shrugged his shoulders.

"Constancia told me she was—she was very beautiful. And very desirable."

He laughed. "Sexy as hell might be a better way of putting it. She came after me like a house afire—Christ, it sounds cold-blooded. But it's the truth. She'd always had a little money, but never enough to keep her happy. And there I was, weary of playing the field, ready to settle down; before I knew it, we were married."

"What went wrong?" Victoria asked softly.

"It's easier to list what didn't." His voice turned grim. "There's no point in pretending I'm not a rich man, Toria. I am. I've homes in Miami, in New York——" He sighed. "Alexandra expected to lead a whirlwind existence, jetting from glamorous party to party. And I—I'd had my fill of all that. What I wanted was peace and quiet."

She smiled a little. "And you found it, on Isla de la Pantera."

"Hell, I wouldn't have bought the island if she'd told me how she felt. But she lied—I don't know why, unless she thought I'd change my mind about living on it after I really owned it. Once we moved into the house, she never let a day go by without reminding me that she hated it." He turned around and leaned back against the railing. "The marriage was a disaster by then anyway. Still, I offered to make a last stab at pulling things together. I said we'd move off the island, try living in San Juan for a while."

"And? What happened?" Victoria asked softly, after Roarke fell silent.

His teeth glinted in the darkness. "It was a classic. I came home from work one night and she was gone. No note, no message, just a whirlwind of whispers left in her wake." His mouth twisted. "She'd run away with a man."

Victoria got to her feet. "But how could she?" she said. "How could she have done such a thing to you and to——"

Roarke laughed. "If you knew her, you wouldn't even ask the question. Alexandra never gives a thought to anyone but herself. She met a guy one night, she fell for him and wham! A week later, she was gone." Roarke turned, leaned his arms on the balcony railing, and gazed out across the dark water. "He took her to Europe—he used her money because I'd seen to it that she couldn't get her hands on mine. A couple of months later, when it was gone, he left her flat."

"It must have been awful for you," Victoria said quietly.

He shrugged his shoulders. "We were divorced by then—my attorneys made quick work of it. She phoned and begged me to take her back, she began to weep—

she was always very good at that—and she asked me if
there wasn't anything in the world that would make me
change my mind. I said no, I even managed to wish her
well—and then I hung up the phone and tried to get on
with my life.''

Victoria walked to his side and laid her hand on his
shoulder. ''By burying yourself in your work and
in——''

''And then, one night, the bell rang. I opened the door
and there was Alexandra.''

''And you took her back.''

Roarke sighed. ''Yes. Hell, what else could I do? It
didn't last long; she was gone again within months.''

She nodded, her heart aching for the man she loved,
while she tried to envisage what kind of woman could
have left him and Susanna behind without so much as
a backward glance. Suddenly, she knew what it must
have cost him to tell her all this. Her heart gave a little
lurch. Maybe—maybe she could tell him about herself.
He would understand. He——

''When I saw Alexandra standing there with an infant
in her arms, when she said, '''Roarke, I want you to
meet your daughter——' ''

Victoria's head came up sharply. ''What?''

''Incredible, isn't it? She'd never even let me know
she'd had my child. Christ, Toria, can you imagine what
it's like to learn something like that without any warning
at all?''

''Do you mean—you didn't know she'd given birth to
Susu?''

''Hell, I didn't even know she'd been pregnant.''
Roarke rubbed his hand across his forehead. ''I took
Susanna from her and looked at her, I kept thinking
that I'd helped create this life——''

Victoria's throat had gone dry. She swallowed, then
swallowed again. ''I can't—I can't believe it, Roarke. It

just—it just doesn't make sense. Are you saying that—that..."

"What I'm saying," he said hoarsely, "is that my sweet, adoring wife had been almost three months pregnant when she ran off with another man." He slammed his hand against the railing. "Can you imagine it, Toria? There she was, in Paris with her lover, and all the time she was carrying my child!"

"Paris." The breath whooshed from Victoria's lungs; for one foolish second she'd almost thought—she'd almost thought... "That's where she had the baby, then?"

Roarke shook his head. "No. That's where her Romeo dumped her. She cut quite a swath after that: Rome, then the States."

"The States." Victoria nodded. There was a terrible numbness rising within her, threatening to engulf her at any second. Concentrate, she told herself fiercely, concentrate on—on those stars. Look at them. Count them. Just keep counting them.

"Yeah." He laughed sharply. "What's it they say? Something about a rolling stone gathering no moss? That was Alexandra's speciality. New York, then Philadelphia—and finally, Chicago."

Victoria took a quick step back. The edge of the chaise longue hit the backs of her legs, and she sank down on to it.

"Chicago, Illinois?" she said stupidly.

Roarke turned toward her, smiling for the first time since he'd begun his story. "That's right. Apparently the Midwest specializes in producing beautiful girls with black hair and blue eyes."

Dear God, Victoria thought, please. Please, no——

"Are you sure?" She cleared her throat. "Are you sure that's where Susanna was born?"

"Alexandra made it sound like the end of the earth." He gave a short, harsh laugh. "I know it's crazy, but hell, it hurts me that I don't even remember where I was or what I was doing the night of her birth. I keep trying to remember. January sixteenth, I say to myself, January sixteenth at seven-thirty." His face darkened, and he slammed his fist on the railing again. "A father should know these things, damn it!"

Victoria made a low, keening sound.

"Toria? Darling, what is it?"

She put her hands to her face. No, she told herself, it was impossible. Coincidence, that was all it was, a strange coincidence that Alexandra Campbell should have given birth to a daughter in Chicago on the very day, at the very hour, that *her* daughter had been born.

"Toria." Roarke knelt beside her and took her into his arms. "Are you ill?"

But it wasn't coincidence. She knew, with sudden terrible clarity, that she had reached the end of her search. Roarke Campbell had, indeed, adopted her daughter— it was just that he didn't know it. He thought Susanna was his child. His wife—his ex-wife—had lied to him; she'd needed a way to get back into his life and she'd found a way, she'd bought a way...

"Victoria!" Roarke's voice was sharp with concern. She looked up slowly and her eyes met his. "What's wrong?"

They both started at the urgent jangle of the telephone. Roarke cursed and reached for it with one hand while he held Victoria close in the curve of his arm. "Yes, Constancia," he said, and then his face closed down. "*Sí,*" he said, "tonight."

She held her breath as he slammed down the receiver and uttered a sharp, ugly word.

"Roarke?" Victoria's heart fell. "Is it—has something happened to Susanna?"

His face was grim. "We have to fly back to the island immediately." He paused, and when he spoke again his voice was cold as steel. "Alexandra is back. But then, a bad penny always turns up."

CHAPTER TEN

VICTORIA stared out of the window as the helicopter swooped across the dark landscape en route to the southern coast of Puerto Rico. There was something almost surrealistic about hurtling through the night this way, in a swift-moving sphere over sleeping villages and quiet towns. She thought of all the people below, lying safe in their beds. Some might be dreaming, but even their worst dreams would end in an instant of awakening.

If only she could expect the same deliverance.

She sighed wearily and leaned her head back. But she couldn't. She was trapped in a nightmare, and she could see no way out of it. If only she'd never let Roarke talk her into staying on Isla de la Pantera. If only she hadn't fallen in love with him.

Victoria closed her eyes. No. There was no sense in that kind of thinking. It wouldn't change anything, and besides, where was she supposed to start? There were far too many "ifs" involved for any one of them to have made a difference, unless you went all the way back to the beginning. If she'd never met Craig, none of this would have happened.

But then there'd have been no Susanna, and it was hard to envisage a world without Susu's innocent face and sweet laughter.

And she'd never have met Roarke, never have had these few weeks of happiness and love at his side and in his arms.

A sob rose in her throat. She put her hand to her mouth, but it was too late. Roarke had heard the muffled sound; he turned to her quickly and took her hand in his.

"Toria? Are you all right?"

She drew a deep breath. No, she wanted to say, I'm not. My life is coming undone, and there's nothing I can do to fix it.

But it was too late. How could she tell him the truth now?

"Sweetheart?"

She sighed as he lifted her hand to his mouth and pressed a kiss into her palm.

"It's nothing," she said. "I just—I have a headache, that's all."

Roarke drew her head down to his shoulder. "You're tired," he said softly. "Why don't you close your eyes and rest until we land?"

She sighed as she curved her body into the comforting warmth of his. Darkness rushed up at them from under the 'copter; they were flying over the sea now, and she tried not to think of what waited just ahead. But, all too soon, the lights of Isla de la Pantera rose on the horizon.

Alexandra Campbell was everything Victoria had imagined she would be. Tall, slender, elegantly dressed in a pale gold washed silk suit the same shade as the stylishly cut hair that framed her high-cheekboned face, Roarke's former wife was a *Vogue* fashion photo come to life. She came down the wide staircase just as Victoria and Roarke stepped through the front door, arms outstretched, looking for all the world as if this were her home and she was welcoming guests into it. She gave Victoria one swift, cold glance, and then she looked at Roarke and smiled.

"Darling," she said in a husky voice, "it's so good to see you again."

Roarke's face was expressionless.

"What are you doing here?" he said in a flat voice.

Alexandra smiled coyly as she moved toward him. "Is that all the greeting I get after such a long time?" She rose on tiptoe and wound her slender arms around his neck. "Hello, darling," she said softly, and she pressed her mouth to his.

Victoria's throat closed. "I—I'll just check on Susanna——"

"No." Roarke's voice was sharp as he reached out and clamped his fingers around her wrist. "Stay here."

She looked at him in mute appeal. "Roarke, you and—and your wife have things to discuss..."

"My ex-wife," he said coldly. "I'll ask you again, Alexandra. What do you want?"

The lovely face twisted into a pout. "Must a woman have a reason for paying a visit to her husband and child?" She let go of him and stepped back a little. Her gaze swept to Victoria, and suddenly the violet eyes gleamed with malice. "Who's your little friend, darling? It's dreadfully rude not to introduce us, you know."

"Alexandra——"

"Very well." She tossed her head so that the shiny fall of hair slipped across her face like silk. "If you won't make the proper introductions, I'll do it myself." Her lips lifted in a bright, false smile and she held out a scarlet-tipped hand rimmed with heavy gold bangles. "How do you do? I'm Alexandra Campbell. And you are...?"

Victoria's heart thudded. My name is Victoria Winters, she wanted to say, I'm the woman whose child you—— But she couldn't; God, she couldn't, not with Roarke standing beside her.

"My name is Victoria Hamilton," she said softly, ignoring the outstretched hand. "I'm Susanna's nanny."

The violet eyes went flat. "What a charming word," she purred. "It has such an old-fashioned quality to it."

Roarke's arm dropped from Victoria's waist and he stepped in front of her. It was such a sweetly chivalrous gesture that it brought a lump to her throat.

"For the last time," he said softly, "why did you come here?"

The blonde's voice chilled. "I gave you my answer, Roarke. I came to see my daughter."

"*Your* daughter?" He laughed. "It's a little late to start thinking of Susanna as *your* daughter, don't you think?"

Alexandra smiled, like a cat contemplating a dish of cream. "It's not a matter of thinking, darling, it's a matter of fact. Susanna is as much mine as she is yours, although we both know how hard you try to forget it."

Roarke's fists clenched. "You don't give a damn for her."

"Of course I do, darling. Why else would I be here?"

"For the same reason you came back before," he said flatly. "For money."

The lovely face hardened. "I'm your wife, Roarke. You owe me——"

"You're not my wife, and I don't owe you a damned thing."

"Ah." Alexandra's voice was soft. "But I'm still Susanna's mother. No divorce can change that, can it?"

Roarke's body stiffened. "If you're feeling maternal stirrings, forget about it. It's too late to try playing at being Susanna's mother again."

The blond woman laughed softly. "Try telling that to the courts, darling. We both know how they feel about a mother's right to her child."

"We've been all through this, Alexandra. You deserted Susu——"

The slim shoulders rose and fell in an easy shrug. "Semantics, darling. I left here because I had no choice; I couldn't go on living with you on this awful island, and it took me years to become whole again. It would make devastating testimony in the hands of a good psychiatrist, don't you think?"

"Alexandra——"

"Of course, there's always the chance you'd win, once we'd gone through all the appeals. I've heard these cases can drag on for years." She sighed dramatically. "It would be difficult for Susanna, I suppose, shuttling from court to court while we battled, but then, she's a sturdy little girl, isn't she?"

"You always were a bitch, weren't you?" Roarke said softly.

"I'm only trying to point out the pitfalls of taking our differences to court, darling, especially since, in the end, you'd probably win." There was a meaningful pause. "After all," she said carefully, "you're the one with all the money."

Roarke shrugged off Victoria's hand. He moved quickly, like the big cat after which his island had been named, closing his hands on Alexandra's shoulders and slamming her back against the wall.

Her voice rose in a shriek. "Let go of me! Damn you, let go or I'll charge you with assault. Just see how much sympathy that brings you in a custody fight."

"Roarke." Victoria's voice trembled. "Roarke, please——"

"Stay out of this, Victoria."

"Roarke." She put her hand on his shoulder; the muscles tensed and bunched beneath her fingers. She whispered his name again, and suddenly she felt his muscles go slack. He drew in a ragged breath, then lifted both hands from his ex-wife's shoulders in a slow, exaggerated gesture, and stepped away from her.

"How much do you want?" he asked softly.

Alexandra crossed her arms over her breasts and massaged her shoulders. "Don't you ever dare try that again, Roarke, or I swear——"

"I asked you a question. How much this time?"

The blond woman blew out her breath, and then she smiled as if nothing had happened.

"You've always been generous, darling. I'll leave it up to you."

"I'll write you a check. I want you out of here."

"No more than I want to leave, believe me. I'll be gone first thing in the morning." The glittering eyes swept from him to Victoria, then back again. "I didn't think you'd be caught by such a mouse, darling," she said with an ugly laugh. "But then, I never did understand your tastes, did I?"

Victoria stood beside Roarke, watching as Alexandra Campbell climbed the stairs and vanished from view. Long minutes passed, and then he turned to Victoria and gathered her to him, holding her so tightly that she could barely breathe.

"You can't imagine how I hate that woman," he said.

Victoria drew in her breath. "Yes, I can," she said softly, and then slowly they went up the stairs together.

Hours later, in the first moments of dawn, Victoria sat up carefully in bed. Roarke lay asleep beside her, his arm curved protectively across her hips. He had finally fallen asleep, but not even sleep had erased the deep furrows from between his brows.

She had not intended to share his bed in this house, certainly not with Alexandra in a room only a few doors down the hall. But Roarke's need for her had burned in his eyes.

"Please, Toria," he'd whispered. "I have to hold you tonight."

How could she have denied him, when being in his arms was what she ached for, too? And so she had gone to him willingly, curling tightly into his embrace, listening to the beat of his heart and the rasp of his breath until finally she'd felt his tension slip away.

But sleep had eluded her. There was too much to think about, too much to anguish over, and now she rose quietly and slipped into his robe. She had to think. It was all so painfully complex. Victoria drew a shuddering breath as she stepped into the silent hallway and closed the door after her. She, and she alone, had the power to wipe away Alexandra Campbell's ugly threats. All she had to do was tell Roarke the truth about his daughter, and his former wife's hold on him would be eliminated forever.

But if she did that, she would break Roarke's heart. In one horrendous moment she would not only tell him the awful truth about herself, she would also destroy everything he'd believed in for the past four years. How could she tell him that the child he adored wasn't his?

Victoria wiped her hand across her eyes as she padded barefoot up the steps to the nursery. There had to be an answer. Maybe, in the silence of Susu's room, she could find it.

She opened the door stealthily, determined not to disturb her daughter's sleep.

Her daughter. The realization sent a shimmer of bittersweet joy through her, and she smiled wistfully as she made her way toward Susanna's bed.

Susu was sleeping on her belly, clutching her teddy bear. Victoria reached out a trembling hand and gently stroked the child's dark curls. What was it Roarke had said? Something about Susu's dark curls and blue eyes being like hers. And they were; why hadn't she seen it before? There was even a similarity about the mouth——

"I had a feeling I might find you here."

Victoria spun around. Alexandra Campbell stood watching her from the open doorway. She was wearing a long black silk negligee; even in the faint glow of the night-light, it was easy to see that she wore nothing else beneath it.

"What—what do you want?"

Alexandra laughed softly. "Just a little chitchat with my daughter's nanny."

The inflection she put on the word made it clear what she thought. Victoria began to tremble. She took one last, lingering glance at Susanna, and then she turned to the other woman and walked toward her.

"I don't want to wake Susanna, Mrs. Campbell. If you insist on carrying on a conversation——"

"Oh, I do. I definitely do."

Victoria nodded. "Then let's go down to the library."

The library was silent and dark. Victoria walked quickly to the french windows and drew open the heavy curtains.

"Now," she said, turning to face Alexandra Campbell, "what is it you want to talk about?"

The blonde leaned lazily against the wall. "You're very much at home here, aren't you?"

Victoria drew herself up. "I told you, I'm Susanna's——"

"Nanny. Yes, so you said." She smiled. "Does my husband lend his robe to all his servants, I wonder?"

Victoria felt her cheeks flame. Don't let her intimidate you, she told herself. This is some kind of game, that's all it is, and you mustn't let her draw you in.

"Mrs. Campbell——"

"How long have you been living with Roarke?" Alexandra demanded in a voice that was suddenly cold.

"I'm not living with him—not in the way you mean."

The other woman laughed. "No? Then why hasn't your bed been slept in, my dear?"

Victoria drew the lapels of the robe together and started toward the door.

"We don't really have anything to discuss," she said carefully, trying to disguise the tremor in her voice. "So if you'll excuse me——"

"Wait, Victoria." Alexandra's voice curled after her like a whip. "I haven't quite finished with you yet."

Victoria stopped in the doorway. Count to ten, she told herself. Now take a deep breath, and just keep remembering that you don't want to do anything that might hurt Roarke.

"I want you out of this house. Immediately."

Victoria closed her eyes, then turned slowly into the room. "That's not your decision to make."

Alexandra looked at her coldly. "My husband——"

"Your *ex*-husband, you mean."

"Roarke's no different from all the rest of the men in the world. He's a fool about women. It doesn't take any effort at all to wind him around your little finger, does it?"

Victoria stuffed her hands into her pockets to keep them from shaking.

"You'd be an expert on that kind of thing, wouldn't you?" she said softly.

Alexandra Campbell smiled coolly. "You're clever, to have come at him this way, I'll give you that."

Victoria stared at her. "What are you talking about?"

The other woman shrugged. "He had quite a reputation as a lady-killer before he met me. Well, why wouldn't he? A man with his looks and his money—he was always quite a catch." She smiled and folded her arms beneath her full breasts. "In those days, he liked his women to be beautiful and sexy." Her gaze swept over Victoria. "But it makes sense that he'd be open to some little homebody now, with Susu to care for and this great mausoleum of an island draining all his energies."

Victoria blinked. "What are you suggesting?"

"It was clever of you, all right. Here's poor Roarke Campbell, still mourning the loss of his wife——"

"Is that what you think? That he misses you?" Victoria laughed. "Believe me, Mrs. Campbell——"

"No," Alexandra said sharply, "*you* believe me, Miss Hamilton." She took a step forward. "Roarke never got over me. What you saw earlier—the rage, the anger— it's all just a cover-up for what he really feels." A smile twisted across her face. "That's how it is when we're in bed together," she said softly, her eyes on Victoria's. "Sometimes, when he makes love to me, he's so passionate that I——"

"You're disgusting." Victoria's voice shook. "And you're a liar. Roarke doesn't love you."

Alexandra laughed. "We mustn't forget our roles here, Victoria." She paused dramatically. "You're just some little thing who saw a way to worm herself into the life of a lonely rich man."

"That's not true. I don't give a damn for his money."

"And you played at caring for Susanna. He must have been touched." Alexandra smiled. "But I'm the real thing, you see. I'm Roarke's wife."

Victoria stared at her. "Go on," she said softly. "I'm sure you're saying all this for a purpose."

Alexandra's eyes narrowed. "Quick, very quick. I mustn't underestimate you." She smiled. "The thing is, I'm bored with traipsing around the world. It might be nice to settle down in one place."

"What—what are you saying?"

The other woman shrugged. "I've been thinking." She walked slowly across the luxurious room, running her hand lightly over the massive pieces of mahogany fur-

niture. "Perhaps I'll stay on here for a few months."
She smiled over her shoulder. "It might be fun."

Victoria stepped forward. "Fun? Walking in and out
of someone's life might be 'fun'? Do you really think
that?" She laughed in disbelief. "Forget it. Roarke won't
give you the chance."

"I can do whatever I like. I thought you understood
that."

"And I think you overestimate your position, Mrs.
Campbell."

Alexandra Campbell laughed. "Perhaps," she said
slyly, "but not my maternal one. I'm Susanna's mother.
That gives me very special power." Her smile fled, and
her voice hardened like steel. "Power you can't possibly
contest."

Victoria felt herself go cold. "How can you do this?
Don't you have any feelings for Roarke? For Susanna?"

The other woman's eyes were frigid. "I want you out
of this house within the hour. *I* am Roarke Campbell's
wife."

"No." Victoria's voice shook. "You are not. Not any
more."

"And I am Susanna's mother. And you are nothing
but a common——"

"You're not that either."

The words fell between them like stones. Alexandra
Campbell paled for an instant, but she recovered quickly.

"I hate to disappoint you, my dear, but a divorce does
not undo motherhood."

Victoria took a step forward. "You're not her
mother." Her voice trembled like a leaf in a wind. "And
you never were."

The other woman stared at her. A muscle ticked suddenly in her eyelid. "What—what nonsense is this?" she
said in an unsteady voice.

"It's the truth, and you and I know it. Susanna's not your child. You—you bought her."

The Campbell woman moved back. "You're crazy. Crazy! I definitely want you out of my house, Miss Hamilton. I don't want a lunatic taking care of my——"

Tears rose in Victoria's eyes. "My name isn't Hamilton. It's Winters. Victoria Winters. I gave birth to a little girl on January sixteenth, four years ago, at Women's Hospital in Chicago at seven-thirty in the evening."

Alexandra Campbell turned white. "What?"

"My doctor said he'd arranged for my baby to be adopted." Victoria's voice broke. "But he lied. He *sold* her, to you. You bought my daughter so you could convince Roarke to take you back."

The beautiful face seemed to be coming apart before Victoria's eyes.

"How did you—how did you find out?"

"I hired a detective. I wanted to see my baby—that's why I came here in the first place."

"You haven't said anything to Roarke?"

"No. No, he doesn't know a thing." Victoria's voice broke.

Alexandra stared at her in silence, then walked to a chair and sat down. Her eyes narrowed as she looked at Victoria, and then she crossed her legs and leaned forward.

"This doesn't change a thing," she said softly. "I still want you off this island within the hour."

Victoria nodded. "Yes," she said wearily. "I'm leaving Isla de la Pantera. But so are you. I'm not going to let you hurt Roarke and Susanna any more."

The woman laughed. "Must I repeat myself? I'm staying." She got to her feet, and her smile faded. "And you can't do a damned thing to stop me."

Victoria lifted her chin in defiance. "Can't I?"

Alexandra smiled. "I know what you're thinking. You think you're going to run right up those steps and tell Roarke this ridiculous story you've made up."

"I'm going to tell him the truth, if that's what it takes to keep you from hurting him again."

"It's the truth you're going to tell him, is it? Well, go on," Alexandra waved her hand toward the door. "You don't see me stopping you, do you? Go on, tell him your story, by all means." Her smile became a sneer. "Tell him. Let him see you for what you really are, Victoria— a slut who dropped a baby the way a bitch drops a litter."

Victoria's breath caught. "No. It wasn't like that."

"Wasn't it? You had a child out of wedlock, and you sold it to the highest bidder."

"That's a lie. I never took any money for my baby."

Alexandra's eyes flashed coldly. "Fifty thousand dollars, that's what I paid for Susanna." She laughed. "Try and convince anybody you didn't see a penny of it."

Victoria felt a chill of apprehension, but it was too late to back down.

"I'll tell Roarke the truth anyway," she said quietly.

"Do it, then. Tell him." The blonde stepped forward, smiling coldly. "Just remember that I'll be here to make certain you tell him the entire story." A smile flickered across her face. "How you didn't just happen to fall into his life. How you sought him out. How you've slept around. How you put a price on what you'd like him to think is the most precious sort of love——"

"Victoria?"

It had to be Roarke; she knew that when she heard him say her name. But his voice sounded hoarse, and when she turned toward the doorway, the twisted look on his face made her breath catch.

"Roarke." She put her hand to her throat. "How—how long have you been standing there?"

He looked from her to Alexandra, then to her again. "What is she talking about, Victoria?"

"She—she——" Victoria's mouth trembled. "Roarke. It's not—it isn't the way she's making it sound."

"Isn't it?" His voice was flat.

"No. No. I—I——"

"Then tell me she was lying." He took a step toward her. "You can do that, can't you?"

Victoria swallowed hard. "Roarke, please. It's not—it's not that simple."

His eyes darkened. "What the hell does that mean? Was she lying, or wasn't she?"

"No. Yes. But not about——"

"No? Yes? What the hell are you saying? It's true, isn't it? You schemed your way into my life, didn't you?" She said nothing, and he moved quickly toward her and grabbed her by the shoulders. "Answer me," he demanded. "Did you come into Campbell's looking for a job that day, or for me?"

"For—for you. But—but..."

"Because I'm Roarke Campbell."

"Yes. But it's not the way it seems."

"She told me everything, darling." Alexandra hurried toward them, her voice soft and filled with concern. "She came to my room a little while ago—she said I'd better get out of your life, that she wasn't going to tolerate any interference. Oh, darling, how awful for you. To have trusted this girl, and all the time she was laying her pathetic little plans."

Victoria stared at Roarke, horrified.

"Roarke. Please, don't believe her."

"Are you saying she's lying?"

"Yes. Of course."

His eyes swept across her face. "Then tell me why you sought me out."

"All right." She ran her tongue along her dry lips. "All right, I will."

Her words faded away and died. Suddenly, the enormity of it all hit her. What could she tell him? That he was not Susanna's father? That would kill him. And what would such a revelation do to Susanna? Roarke was the only father the little girl had ever known. She had already forfeited the right to raise her own child; to deny her little girl Roarke's love would be the cruelest act of all.

"I'm waiting," he said softly.

Victoria looked at him. The tears that had risen in her eyes began spilling down her cheeks.

"I—I have no answers," she whispered.

She thought, for one moment, that he might kill her. His hands slid to her throat; she felt the press of his fingers in the hollow where her pulse leaped, and then, suddenly, he flung her from him.

"Get out of my house," he muttered.

"Roarke——"

"Get out! Do you hear me?"

Alexandra Campbell moved to Roarke's side. "It's all right, darling," she said softly. She touched his cheek, his shoulder, then his outstretched hand. Slowly, he lowered his arm and curved it tightly around her, his fingers splaying just below the lush curve of her breast.

It was the last thing Victoria saw before she flew from the room, and it was a memory that she knew would be stamped into her mind forever: Roarke, looking as cold as she had ever seen him, and Alexandra Campbell, standing beside him with a smile of glittering triumph on her face.

CHAPTER ELEVEN

IT CAME as no shock to find that life was filled with unimaginable cruelty. Things happened to people that seemed, at first, to be insufferable. But you *could* survive, you *did* survive. Victoria had learnt that first-hand.

She kept telling herself that as the helicopter carried her away from Isla de la Pantera. It was all she thought about as she took her seat in the plane that would carry her back to Chicago.

You can get through this, a little voice inside her was whispering.

Could she? Her life had been shattered, it lay in pieces all around her, and she couldn't imagine how she could pick up the pieces and put them back together again. She had lost everything—*everything*: Roarke, Susanna, and her self-respect. How could she possibly overcome that?

She remembered him as he had looked in those last minutes: the dark coldness in his eyes, the tormented grimace of his mouth. Her throat tightened. She'd kept the truth about herself from him because she'd been terrified of losing his love, and now she'd lost it anyway. For the rest of her life she'd remember the way he'd looked at her, with first pain and then hatred blazing in his face.

Roarke, she thought brokenly, Roarke, how I love you. If only there'd been time to find a way to set the past aside.

"Miss? Are you okay?"

Victoria looked up. The flight attendant was standing in the narrow aisle, leaning toward her with more than polite concern.

"Yes," she said, "I'm fine."

"You sure? If you feel sick or something——"

"No. No, really. I'm all right."

The girl hesitated. "Well, if you need anything——"

"I'll let you know. Thank you."

Victoria glanced at the woman beside her as the attendant made her way up the aisle. The woman was watching her cautiously, and Victoria tried to smile reassuringly. But it didn't seem to work very well, because her seatmate quickly opened a magazine and buried her nose in it.

Victoria sat back and folded her hands tightly in her lap. All right, she told herself, that's enough of that. You have a long trip ahead of you, and a bus ride to Broadwell, and you're not going to make it if you fall apart at the seams. Think about something. No, not Roarke. Not him. If you think about him, you'll be lost.

Dr. Ronald. Yes, that was who she'd think about. The bastard's name was enough to make her stomach knot, but it was a better pain than the one she felt in her heart. She made mental lists of all the things she would say to him, the questions she wanted answered, and suddenly she knew that she would never rest until she confronted him. It wouldn't be easy—he'd retired and moved away not long after her mother's death. In fact, it killed her to think that she'd been one of those who'd stopped by to wish the old man well. But she'd find him. She'd find him, and then she'd pour out her anger and her pain. He had done something to her that no one had the right to do, and she wanted to be sure he knew that he hadn't got away with it.

*   *   *

O'Hare Airport was crowded with travelers returning from winter vacations. Victoria heard snatches of cheerful conversation as she made her way to the baggage area.

"...never saw a beach like that before, did you?"

"...such a good time! The people, and the hotel——"

Her fellow travelers were already reliving the memories of their vacations in the sun. Victoria's mouth trembled. She wanted only to forget, not to remember. If she remembered, how would she face the empty years that stretched ahead?

And yet, how could she not remember? She had never known such happiness as she'd known the past weeks, and she had lost it all. She would never hold Susu in her arms again, never watch her grow, never hear her laughter.

And Roarke. How could she not think about Roarke? He was imprinted on her soul and on her heart; she could hear his voice, see his face, feel the touch of his hands. Everything he was had become part of her.

And now he hated her, *hated* her! Dear God, no matter what she had done, she didn't deserve that. It was agony to know that she would never see him again, but to know that he believed Alexandra's ugly lies was even worse.

A sob escaped her lips. The couple standing beside her at the carousel looked at her, then at each other. She turned and walked quickly to the other end of the revolving belt, and when her one worn suitcase came into view—it was all she'd needed, since she'd left behind all the things Roarke had bought her—she snatched it up and hurried from the terminal.

She was almost dizzy with fatigue by the time the bus dropped her off in front of the dark post office in Broadwell. The little town, wrapped in the icy silence of late winter, seemed foreign after the warmth and brightness of Isla de la Pantera. But it was home, and it had never looked as welcome as it did now. Victoria hoisted her suitcase, ducked her head against the wind, and trudged through the frigid streets to her apartment.

The tiny apartment was cramped and stuffy. How close she'd come to giving it up, she thought as she dragged her suitcase into the bedroom and dumped it on a chair. Roarke had urged her to cancel her lease and put her things in storage when she'd first agreed to stay on as Susu's nanny.

"I'll take care of all the arrangements," he'd said.

But something had urged her not to cut all her ties to home, and now, as she turned on the kitchen light and filled the kettle for tea, she was very glad she hadn't. She was weary to the bone with the kind of numbing exhaustion that was not so much physical as it was emotional, and she knew that to have had to make any kind of decision now, even one about where to spend the night, would have been overwhelming.

What she needed, she thought as she pulled off her clothing and fell into bed, was to empty her mind of everything for a few days. And then—and then——

Darkness rolled up and swallowed her.

She lost touch with reality. The one thing that had seemed important—locating Dr. Ronald—faded beside her endless need for sleep. Time passed; she knew it did because sometimes she awoke to sunshine, sometimes to night. She ate when she was hungry, taking tins from the kitchen cupboard without reading labels, eating tuna or beans or soup or whatever food came tumbling out. It was all nourishment, and what did it matter what anything tasted like?

The only thing that counted was sleep. Sleep took away the pain of all that she'd lost, and it brought her dreams—sweet, wonderful dreams—of Roarke and of the time she had spent with him.

Then, one day, as Victoria turned from the sink to put the kettle on to boil, she looked out of the kitchen window. The previous spring, in a rare moment of whimsy, she had bought a flat of pansies and planted them in a window box just outside.

"They're so beautiful," she'd said, smiling at the florist, "I just hope they survive."

"They will," he'd said positively. "They're tough as nails. Just don't expect them to come back, miss. They'll bloom this season, and then they're done."

She set the kettle down and opened the window. Spring had come to the land; the scent of green growing things was in the air, but the miracle that had caught Victoria's eye was the one unfolding in the window box. No one had told the pansies that they'd never see a second summer. Soft green shoots were pushing up through the soil, heralding the velvety flowers that would soon appear.

Victoria touched the delicate shoots in wonder, and then turned slowly and looked around her kitchen, seeing for the first time the dishes piled in the sink, the empty tins overflowing the garbage can. She moved slowly through the apartment, her fingers leaving trails in the dust that covered all the furniture, inhaling air that smelled of staleness and despair. When she reached the bedroom mirror, she stopped dead.

"Dear God," she whispered.

Her hair hung in unruly tangles. She was wearing a nightgown that looked as if she'd slept in it for days. She looked, she thought as she walked slowly toward her reflection, like a woman who had given up.

But she couldn't give up. She never had before, despite whatever life had dished out. And wasn't there something she'd wanted to do? Dr. Ronald. Yes, that was it, she wanted—hell, she *insisted*—on facing him and getting some answers.

Victoria pulled off her nightgown and stepped into the shower. She scrubbed her body and her hair and let the water sluice over her until she began to feel alive. Then she slipped on the white cotton blouse, black twill skirt, and flat-heeled oxfords that was as close to a uniform as waitresses who worked for Bernie ever wore. One last deep breath, and she stepped out into the world again.

Bernie was at the open cash register when she pushed open the door to the Route 66 Café. If he was surprised to see her, he certainly didn't show it.

"Son of a gun," he said laconically, "just look what the wind blew this way."

Victoria smiled. "Hello, Bernie. How've you been?"

"Can't complain," he said, shutting the cash drawer. "We were talkin'" about you, just the other day." He leaned his meaty forearms on the counter and gazed at her. "Couple of customers and me, that is. We figured maybe you liked it so much you'd decided to stay down there, in—what was it—the Bahamas?"

She shook her head. "Puerto Rico."

"Yeah, well, one island's the same as another, right?"

Victoria's mouth trembled. "No," she said softly, "not—not really. They're very different."

Bernie straightened and took a wet rag from behind him. "So, what're you doin'" here?" He made a desultory pass at the counter with the rag. "You sayin'" hello? Or are you lookin'" for a job?"

"A job," she said levelly. "If you can use me."

He shrugged his shoulders. "Can always use a good waitress. Only thing is, Lurleen took your shift. You wanna work, you take the four to closing."

"Four to midnight?" She blew out her breath. Why not? She was almost broke, and the tips would be better on the late shift. Besides, what did it matter when she worked? She had hours to fill and no life to fill them with. "Sure, that's fine with me. When do I start?"

Bernie grinned. "Is today too soon?"

It was hard, the first couple of hours. Victoria's feet ached as if they'd been away too long from these hard tile floors. She singed her fingers the first time she picked up a plate that had sat too long under the heat lamp, and she was careless when she leaned over the grill so that hot grease splattered up and pocked her blouse.

Bernie's bushy brows rose. "You okay?"

She nodded as she rubbed impatiently at the spots. "Fine."

"What'd you do down there in them islands?" her boss said as he slid a spatula under a hamburger and flipped it. He laughed. "Musta been pretty good to make you forget your way around a hot grill."

Victoria looked away from him. "It just—it feels as if I've been away a long time," she said softly.

He grinned. "Musta been like Paradise, huh?"

The seconds ticked away before she trusted herself enough to answer. "Yes," she said finally, "that's exactly what it was. Paradise."

The other waitresses wanted to hear all about the Caribbean. "Is it really as pretty as they say?" one sighed over coffee during the after-supper lull. "Palm trees, white sand, sunshine——"

"And gorgeous guys," the other girl said. "Come on, Victoria, tell us you met some Prince Charming on the beach."

Victoria's smile was uncertain. "I—I met a lot of people."

The first girl made a face. "Yeah, those TV ads lie. You know, the ones that make it look like you're gonna

find the man of your dreams on one of them islands."
She drank the last of her coffee, sighed, and got to her
feet. "There ain't no happy endings in this world, and
that's the truth."

Victoria swallowed and looked down into her cup.
"No," she said softly, "there aren't."

By the time she was halfway through that first shift
she felt as if she had never been away. Her feet had gone
from hurting to feeling numb, the way they always had
in the past. She smiled politely at jokes she'd heard a
million times before, stepped away easily from the yahoos
who didn't know where their hands belonged, offered
the same polite, "Thanks, but my boyfriend wouldn't
approve," to the inevitable offer to take her "some-
wheres nice" after her shift ended.

Time passed. She worked hard, taking on extra shifts
for whoever needed time off. Working was good for her;
after a while she began to feel almost human again—if
she didn't worry about the hollow place in her breast
where her heart had once been. But she didn't expect
that to change. The best she could hope for was to
survive, like the pansies. But to bloom as they would—
that was not about to happen.

The days became weeks which became months, and
the things that had happened on Isla de la Pantera began
to seem unreal. Could she have ever been so happy? It
didn't seem possible. But it had happened, she knew it
when she woke up crying from her dreams in the middle
of the night, or when she'd look up suddenly and see a
man with dark hair and broad shoulders.

Roarke, her anguished soul would whisper—but, of
course, it never was Roarke. It was never even anyone
like him, for how could there ever be another man to
take his place?

By now, she knew where the doctor was. He'd moved
to Florida, Bernie mentioned in passing.

"One of them retirement communities," he said, naming it.

Victoria made a mental note of the place. It would take months to save enough money to fly down and confront the doctor, but she was determined to do it. And then, one hot summer evening, when business was at its slowest, fate stepped into her life. She was leaning on the counter, trying to concentrate on the day's newspaper, when she looked up and saw Dr. Ronald come through the door.

She thought, at first, that he might be an apparition. He looked old and tired, and there was an unhealthy pallor to his skin. She put her order pad on the counter and glanced around her. The other waitresses were at a booth in the rear, drinking Cokes and gossiping. Bernie was somewhere in the back, inventorying supplies.

She took a deep breath, then stepped around the counter into the aisle.

"Dr. Ronald?" she said softly.

He smiled hesitantly. "Yes? Who is—Victoria." His smile faded, and she thought he looked suddenly furtive. But he drew himself together quickly and held out his hands. "Victoria, my dear. What a lovely surprise. I'd forgotten you worked here. My wife and I were just passing through, and——"

"Dr. Ronald." She moved toward him. "I can't believe it's you."

"It's wonderful to see you too, dear. How have you been?"

Her hands were shaking so much that she had to put them into her pockets. She licked her lips nervously.

"I want to talk to you, Doctor."

The old man shook his head and took a step back. "I wish I could chat, my dear, but I'm in a devil of a rush. I only stopped in to use the——" He stared at her as she clutched his arm and drew him out of the door.

"Victoria. What is this about? I told you, I'm pressed for time."

It was more than just her hands that were shaking now. She was trembling from head to foot. Now that the moment was here her anger, her rage, overcame her.

"How could you?" she whispered.

He paled. "How could I what? I don't know what you're talking about."

But he did. She could see it in his face. "Don't pretend," she said harshly. "I know the truth, Doctor. I've seen my daughter."

Ronald's jaw grew slack. "What do you mean?"

"I mean," she said, staring into his face, "that I know what you did. You sold my baby. *Sold* her, as if she were a—a dog..."

"She was adopted," he said quickly. "It was all legal."

"Since when is selling babies legal?"

"Victoria, you musn't make such swift judgements."

"You lied about everything, Doctor. You told me you'd met the parents. But you never did."

The old man seemed to shrink inside his clothes. "Their attorney assured me they would be devoted to the baby, Victoria. The money was a gesture of their commitment."

"The money was for you," she hissed, "because what you were doing was against the law. How could you have done it?"

His defenses crumpled in the face of her anger. Sighing, he told her the story, his old man's eyes rheumy with remorse. It was the first time he'd ever done anything like it, he said. He was old, his practice was failing. His wife had become ill. It was a story that might have moved Victoria if the doctor's dishonesty hadn't so horribly distorted her life.

"The lawyer who handled the adoption swore the child would go to a wonderful home," he said, his voice unsteady. "And the money was a—a fee, your mother's care was quite..." His words fell to a whisper. "All I had to do was—was make certain the birth certificate had the proper names on it." He paused, then ran his tongue along his lips. "It wasn't—it wasn't so terrible. You couldn't keep the child, and she had a good home." A dart of fear flashed across his face and settled in his eyes. "What—what are you going to do?"

She stared at him as she slumped back against the wall. What *could* she do? If she went to the law, she would only involve Roarke in a scandal, and to what end? He was Susanna's father; it was the one joy left in her empty life, the knowledge that her little girl was being raised by the only man she would ever love.

Still, the doctor shouldn't get off the hook that easily. He needed to worry a little, if only as partial payment for the pain he'd caused.

Victoria's eyes fastened on his. "I'm not sure," she said slowly. "I could go to the authorities."

The old man's breathing quickened. "You can't."

"I don't know," she said with quiet defiance.

"You can't," he said again, his hands shaking. "You signed the papers. It's all legal. There's nothing you can do."

"Can't I?"

She swung on her heel and walked away from him. He was sweating, and it was good to see. Maybe a little honest sweat would help cleanse his soul.

She had the next two days off, and for the first time since she'd returned from Isla de la Pantera she didn't spend them moping around her apartment. She went out to the park instead, her face turned up to the summer sunshine—until a tall man with dark hair came trotting down the lane toward her with a child perched on his shoulders. Tears flooded her eyes with a fierce swiftness, and she rose from the bench where she'd been sitting and began a numb, mindless walk that ended at her apartment, hours later.

When would she forget? she wondered, but she knew the answer. She would never forget, not as long as she drew breath.

For some reason she began to lose ground after the incident in the park. She had never stopped dreaming of Roarke, but now each dream was filled with anguish; she awoke with her eyes red-rimmed, her pillow damp. She began to imagine seeing him everywhere. He was always coming down the street toward her, or standing just ahead of her in the line at the market, or smiling at her across the counter in the café.

That was why she wasn't really surprised when she thought she saw him standing framed in the open door of her apartment one morning. The bell had rung and she'd pulled the door open expecting it to be her landlady come to talk about a leak in the kitchen. But it wasn't. Even with the sun in her eyes she could see that the figure in the doorway was male, tall and broad of shoulder.

Her heart kicked against her ribs, the way it always did, and she took a deep breath to quiet it down.

"Yes?" she said with a hesitant smile, and then the figure moved—and she saw—oh, God—she saw that it really was him.

It was Roarke.

CHAPTER TWELVE

SHE stood staring at him, her mouth half-open, her eyes wide and stunned. She had dreamed of him a thousand times, thought of him that many times more, but she had never imagined she would see him again. To throw open the door and find him here, on her narrow landing, was so unbelievable that at first she just couldn't quite grasp it.

"Roarke?" she said finally, in a rusty croak.

"Victoria." His voice was coolly polite, which was exactly the way he looked. He was wearing a navy pinstripe suit with a white shirt and maroon striped tie. He looked, she thought wildly, as if he were about to conduct a board meeting right here in her living room. When she said nothing, his brows rose. "May I come in?"

Her tongue felt glued to the roof of her mouth, but it didn't matter. His question had been one of form, not meaning; the words were hardly out of his mouth before he stepped past her into the tiny entryway of her apartment. She stared after him, transfixed, while her brain made fevered attempts to understand what was happening.

Roarke was here, in Broadwell. But that was preposterous.

Another step brought him into the center of her living room. She watched as he looked around him, his distaste for his surroundings evident in the slight hunch of his shoulders, and then he turned to face her.

"I haven't inconvenienced you, I hope."

His face was as expressionless as his voice. But he looked different. Older. Wearier. There were new lines fanning out from the corners of his eyes, deeper ones etched beside his mouth, and there were light threadings of silver at his temples.

Oh, but the sight of him was wonderful. It was——

"...would have telephoned first, but I didn't think of it until I'd reached your street, and I decided to ring your bell and see if you were in. I hope that's all right, Victoria."

"No, that's okay. I just——" She swallowed. "Roarke? What—what are you doing here?"

His eyes turned cold. "Perhaps you'd like to shut the door before I answer that."

"The door?" she asked stupidly.

"Yes." His voice was grim. "We've a private matter to discuss."

She stared at him for a few seconds longer, and then she pushed the door closed. When she turned around again, Roarke had walked to the narrow pine table that stood near the window. She watched as he reached into his breast pocket and pulled out an envelope.

"My attorneys drew this up," he said, turning to her and holding the envelope out. "I asked them to put it in terms that would be clear to a layman, but if you've any questions..."

Victoria swallowed dryly. "I do," she said. She cleared her throat. "Have questions, I mean."

He smiled coolly. "Really? But you've yet to read the document."

"I meant—how have you been, Roarke? Are you—are you well?"

His eyes went flat. "I've been fine. Now, if you'd just——"

"And Susanna?" She took a step toward him. "Is she—is she well, too?"

His mouth curved like a bow. "Your concern is touching, Victoria. Now, if you'll please read this——"

"Is something wrong with Susu?" Her voice trembled.

"No, of course not. She's fine."

She breathed a sigh of relief. "Good." She gave him a shaky smile. "That's good. You scared me for a minute. I was afraid——"

"She still asks for you."

Her head came up sharply. He was watching her with icy calmness, but there was a betraying shadow in his voice. He still hates me, she thought, and a tremor went through her.

"Does she?" She tried to smile again, but she couldn't quite pull it off. "Well, I—I think of—of..." To her horror, her voice broke. She turned away blindly and wiped her hands across her eyes. "Would you—would you like coffee, or..."

"This isn't a social call."

Victoria closed her eyes. "No," she said softly, "no, of course not. I just——" She paused, then slowly turned and stared at him. "Roarke? How did you find me?"

His lips drew back from his teeth. "It wasn't difficult. Broadwell's a small town."

"Yes, but——"

"And there's just one Victoria Winters in the telephone book."

Her breath caught. "Winters? You—you know my name is...?"

"I'm afraid I'm rather pressed for time." He spoke brusquely as he walked toward her, the envelope held in his outstretched hand. "Read this, see if it meets with your approval, and let's have done with it."

She took the envelope from him and opened it. "What is it?" she asked softly, her eyes on his face.

Roarke's nostrils flared. "It's self-explanatory, I think."

She bent her head over the papers that fluttered out. Legal terms leaped at her, heavy with stilted verbiage. "Party of the first part'...'attests and hereby swears'...'agrees and guarantees in perpetuity''——

She looked up, frowning. "What is this, Roarke?"

He gave her a thin smile. "There's something clipped to the next page that will make a lot more sense to you."

Victoria turned the page over, her eyes on his face. "I still don't——" Her breath caught as she looked down at the document in her hands. There was a check attached to it, a check made out to her in an amount that had too many zeros to even approximate a real number. She stared at it in silence, then lifted her head and looked at Roarke. "What is this?" she whispered.

"What does it look like?" he asked harshly.

She laughed uncertainly. "I don't know. That's why I..."

"Did you read the document?" Roarke strode toward her and snatched the papers from her hand. He scanned them impatiently, then held the last page before her and pointed to the final paragraph. "This is the part that matters, where you swear to give up all future rights and claims to Susanna in exchange for..."

She staggered back as if his words had been blows. "What?"

Roarke's head rose. He stared at her through dark, cold eyes. "You won't get a dime unless you sign it, as is," he said flatly. "And if you're thinking of holding out for more——"

Her eyes flew to his face and swept across it. He knew! Dear Lord, he knew.

"...not a chance in hell of getting her back. If you try, I'll see to it you spend the rest of your life in court—or in jail. Do you understand me, Victoria?"

Her heart leaped. "You—you know, then?" she whispered.

"That you gave birth to my daughter?" His mouth twisted. "Yes. I know."

She stepped away from him and stretched out her hand, feeling for the couch she knew must be behind her, and then she sank down onto it.

"But how? Did Alexandra tell you?"

Roarke laughed harshly. "The only thing Alexandra ever told me about Susanna's birth was some long, heart-rendering tale about her terrible hours in labor."

Victoria swallowed. "Then how did you find out?"

"Dr. Ronald contacted me."

She stared at him. "I don't understand."

He shrugged his shoulders. "He telephoned me a few days ago. Apparently, you panicked him. He was afraid you were going to go to the authorities and bring criminal charges against him and the attorney who set up the adoption. He told me you were going to sue to regain custody of Susanna; he thought he'd better warn me." He drew a breath, and his face seemed to draw in on itself. "Of course, he had no idea I didn't know Susu had been adopted. That was a little secret Alexandra had shared only with the shyster who set it up."

Victoria got to her feet. "Roarke," she said softly, her eyes on his twisted face, "I'm so sorry you had to find out like that. I didn't want you to——"

"No, of course you didn't. You wanted to spring it on me yourself." His mouth thinned. "You really had the old fool convinced, Victoria. He was certain you were going to serve me with papers."

She shook her head. "No. No, I'd never have done that."

He grinned. "Naturally not. But the threat of it would have done the trick, wouldn't it? I'd have shelled out whatever you wanted to keep you from trying to get Susu back."

Victoria's face paled. "Is that—is that what you think?"

He gave her a look so filled with contempt that it made her stomach rise into her throat.

"It's what I know," he said coldly.

"Roarke——"

"You almost had it all, didn't you? You came to Puerto Rico to blackmail me."

"No. That's a lie!"

"Don't waste your breath, Victoria. Once I knew the truth about—about my daughter, it was painfully easy to see through your scheme. The fifty thousand you got when you sold her wasn't enough; you wanted more. So you flew to Puerto Rico to blackmail me into giving you money." He drew a harsh breath. "But then you had a better idea. If you got me to fall in love with you you'd have it all. Hell, why settle for a one-time payoff when you could put yourself in a spot where you'd get a hell of a lot more?"

Her hand flew to her throat. God, what he thought of her! He believed her capable of anything—of the most vile acts imaginable. But how could she blame him, when she had lied to him every step of the way, when she had committed the vilest act of all by giving up her own baby?

A sob burst from her throat and she swung away from his hate-filled eyes. She had spent four years telling herself that she had done the right thing by giving Susu up for adoption, and perhaps she had. But she had never, in her heart, really believed it. And now she deserved everything that had happened. She deserved it all. The pain, the anguish, the hopelessness.

But Susanna deserved better.

"Roarke?" She inhaled deeply, then slowly let out her breath. "You don't—you don't feel differently about Susu now that you know, do you?"

He moved swiftly toward her, his face contorting as he grabbed hold of her shoulders.

"What kind of bastard do you think I am?" he growled. "Susanna is my daughter, and I love her. Hell, I love her even more, now that I——"

He fell silent, but she knew what he was thinking. He loved Susu more than ever now that he knew she had been abandoned by her own flesh and blood. Tears rose in her eyes and streamed down her cheeks.

"Victoria." His voice was rough. "Will you sign the papers? Will you give up all claims to Susanna forever?"

She wanted to tell him that she had no claims, that she had left Isla de la Pantera rather than risk breaking his heart. She wanted to tell him, too, that she would never stop loving him, that the few weeks they had spent together would be the memories that would warm her through the empty years that stretched ahead.

But it was too late to tell him any of it. Instead, she held out her hand and took the document from him, walked to the table and picked up a pen.

"Yes," he said in a harsh whisper, "I suppose it was foolish to think you wouldn't."

She scrawled her name quickly, unable to see the letters for the tears in her eyes, and then she straightened up and held the papers out to him. His face was blurred, but she could see him looking at her, waiting as if for some special message, and then, slowly, he reached out, took the document from her, and stuffed it into his pocket.

"Goodbye, Victoria," he said hoarsely.

She watched as he walked to the door, and then, suddenly, she glanced at the table.

"Wait," she cried.

Roarke turned quickly. "What is it?"

She held out her hand. "You forgot this." He stared at the check, and she took a step toward him.

"It's too late for that," he said, watching her. "You signed the agreement; I'm not going to up the price now."

"I don't want your money." Her eyes, and her voice, were steady. "You can't buy and sell a child, Roarke."

His hands knotted into fists. "If you're thinking of fighting that document, I assure you it's legal and binding."

"Your attorneys would know more about that than I would. I'm only telling you that I never sold my daughter, and I'm not about to do it now."

Roarke stalked toward her. "All right, let's have it all. What is it you want?"

What did she want? It was such a simple question, but the answer to it was complex beyond imagining. She wanted everything—her self-respect, her child, and most of all, Roarke's love.

A miracle. That was what she wanted. Victoria's glance slipped past him to the window and the flowers nodding on the ledge outside. The flowers had endured despite the fate predicted for them. But that had been no miracle, it had been survival.

She was a survivor, too. Hadn't she proved that time and time again? She would not bloom without love but, if she at least recovered her sense of worth, she could endure. Surely that wasn't asking too much.

Her chin lifted. And then there was Susanna. Some day her little girl would ask about the mother who had given her up for adoption. When the time came she was entitled to know the truth.

"Well?" Roarke was watching her impatiently, his hands on his hips. "What is it you want now, Victoria?"

She took a steadying breath. "My self-respect," she said quietly.

He laughed. "That's touching, but the request comes a little late. You gave that up when you gave away your child."

"No." She snapped out the word, hurling it at him like a stone. "I never gave her away, Roarke, not the way you mean. I loved my baby despite the fact that I— I despised her father."

His expression darkened. "I'm not really interested in hearing about your tawdry little affair. You did what you did, and you paid the price."

"Yes." Her eyes met his. "I did. I was—I was just a fool, that's all; I thought Craig cared for me, when all he wanted was to use me."

Victoria drew a breath. Roarke's eyes were cold; for a second, she wanted to retreat into silence and let him walk off without hearing the rest. But she had gone too far to stop now. She turned slowly and walked to the window. Maybe if she didn't have to watch the hatred in his eyes she could summon the strength to finish what she'd begun.

"When I found out I was pregnant," she said steadily, "I wanted to die. What could I offer a child? I had no money, no future. I'd been raised without a father, by a mother who had to scrape to make it through each day. I didn't want to condemn my baby to that kind of life."

"A story that brings tears to my eyes," he said sarcastically. "You ought to offer it to a soap opera. They could probably use it."

His words cut her to the bone, but she was determined to go on.

"And then there was my mother," she said. "She was failing rapidly by then; how could I tell her that I was pregnant? It would have killed her to know that I was repeating the tragedy of her own life." She put her hands on the sill and stared blindly out of the window. "I went to Dr. Ronald for advice. And he——"

"He gave you the perfect way out." Roarke's tone was harsh. "You could salve your conscience and pick up more money than you'd ever dreamed of in one easy deal.''

"Damn you, Roarke!" Victoria spun to face him, her eyes glittering with proud, unshed tears. "Not everyone puts a price tag on things, don't you understand that yet? I told you, I never even knew money changed hands until Alexandra told me. She paid it to Dr. Ronald; he was the one who..." Her voice broke when she saw the look of cool disbelief on his face. She snatched the check from him and shredded it into a dozen pieces. "There," she said fiercely. "That's what I think of your money, Roarke Campbell. And if you don't believe me, you can—you——"

Sobs burst from her throat. She stared at him in horror, then turned away and buried her face in her hands, weeping as she had not wept since she had left him.

"That's a touching story, Victoria, but you've left something out. If you didn't want money for Susanna, why did you come to Puerto Rico?" His hands clasped her shoulders and he forced her to turn toward him. His face was blurred through her tear-dampened lashes, but she could see the cold anger etched in every harsh line. "And why did you worm your way into my life, if not to blackmail me?"

"No! I never——"

"So you keep insisting. But I don't believe you. You came after me for money." Roarke's mouth thinned; something like pain flashed across his face. "And once you realized I might be susceptible to you, you decided to gamble for the entire pot."

Victoria gave a choked laugh. "I didn't even know Susanna was mine until you told me the story of her birth that last night." Roarke's eyes narrowed. "Ask the good doctor, if you don't believe me," she said, her voice bitter. "Or ask Alexandra—if you can ever get her to speak the truth."

His lips drew back from his teeth. "It's going to be tough to ask her anything. I sent her packing half an hour after you left Isla de la Pantera."

She caught her breath. "Did you?"

He nodded grimly. "Yes. And now that I know she has no hold on Susanna I don't plan on ever seeing her again." His eyes swept over her face. "All right," he said slowly, "let's just assume, for the moment, that you didn't come to Puerto Rico to make a fast buck. Why did you, then?"

Victoria sighed deeply. "It's—it's not easy to explain," she said softly. "You see, I'd never stopped thinking about my baby. What did she look like? Was she happy? What kind of family did she have?" She turned away from him again, not wanting him to see the tears rising in her eyes. He was still holding her and somehow, despite the fact that she knew he despised her, the feel of his hands on her gave her the courage to go on. "I only wanted a glimpse of the people who'd adopted her, and maybe—just maybe—a glimpse of my little girl, too."

Her voice broke. In the following silence, she heard the rasp of Roarke's indrawn breath.

"So you came to Campbell Enterprises looking for me?"

"Yes. I had your name, but not your address. I was—I was going to follow you, you see, and—and..." She sighed. "But I followed the wrong man. He wore glasses, he had thinning hair——"

Roarke turned her toward him. For the first time, a smile flickered across his face.

"Tennyson," he said, "my comptroller. It's not a flattering description, but it's accurate."

"When you told me you were Roarke Campbell I was stunned. By the time we reached Isla de la Pantera I was sure I was on a wild-goose chase." She swallowed dryly. "And then I saw Susu."

"And you saw there was a resemblance." Roarke's voice roughened. "I saw it, but I thought it was just—just some special magic that you and Susu should both have soft dark curls and eyes like bits of the sky."

"I didn't see it, not then." Her voice faltered. "But I did ask Constancia if Susu was adopted."

"And she said she wasn't."

"Of course." Victoria let out a shaky breath. "It didn't matter. I'd already realized it had been wrong for me to go looking for my baby. I had no right to search for her, or even to—to ache for her..."

Roarke's hands spread on her shoulders. "Giving her away must have been awful," he said softly.

She looked up at him through a sudden veil of tears. "Oh, yes," she whispered. "More awful than you'll ever know. But there was no other way. I—I don't expect you to understand."

He sighed as his arms closed around her. She began to weep quietly, and he brought her head to his chest and stroked her hair.

"I do understand, Toria. You did what you had to do."

"I love Susanna," she murmured. "I'd never hurt her. You must believe that."

"Yes," he said in a voice gone strangely gruff, "I do."

"That was part of the reason I didn't take Alexandra up on her dare, even though I was tempted."

"What dare?"

"She taunted me that night. Go on, she said, tell Roarke everything—but she knew I couldn't, even though it would have ended her hold on you."

Roarke cleared his throat. "Because you didn't want to hurt Susanna?" he said in an oddly quiet voice.

She nodded. "And—and for other reasons."

"Toria." His hands cupped her face and lifted it gently. "What other reasons?"

"Because——" Because I love you, she thought, but what was the point in saying it, when he wouldn't believe it? "Because I knew how much Susu meant to you. I knew it would hurt you terribly to learn the truth."

Roarke smiled a little. "It did hurt, at first. But then I thought, hell, biology isn't the only thing that makes for parenthood. Even I'm not fool enough to think that."

"Then—your love for Susu hasn't changed?"

"I told you it hadn't." He hesitated, and he lifted her face another inch until he was looking into her eyes. "I love her even more."

"That's good. I'm so glad——"

"Don't you want to know why?" He smiled as he traced her mouth with his finger. "I love her even more," he said softly, "because she's a part of you." Victoria's heart seemed to stop beating as Roarke's arms went around her. "God, when I think of how close I came to losing you—I love you, Toria," he said fiercely. "I've never stopped loving you."

She stared at him, wanting desperately to believe. But she was afraid. If it wasn't true—if he didn't love her——

"How?" she whispered, her eyes searching his. "How could you love me, when you thought—when you believed me capable of——"

"Forgive me for that, my love." He kissed her mouth, her damp eyelids, her temples. "I never believed it, not in my heart. No matter what Alexandra said, no matter what Ronald told me, my heart kept reminding me of what I really knew about you: that you were warm and sweet and kind." He smiled and kissed her again, his mouth lingering on hers. "The trouble is, I'm not a man who's used to listening to his heart. If I had, maybe I wouldn't have been such a damned fool."

Tears spilled down Victoria's cheeks. "Oh, Roarke——"

"Tell me you love me still," he said. "Tell me I didn't kill your love when I sent you away that night."

Victoria laughed and sniffed back her tears. "You could never do that," she said. "I'll always love you, Roarke. Always."

He drew her close and silenced her with a long, sweet kiss. When they finally drew apart they were both trembling.

"There's just one problem," he said finally, reaching into his pocket. His brow furrowed as he drew out the contract she'd signed. "You're right, you know. Agreements like this aren't worth the paper they're written on."

Victoria's mouth trembled. "I told you, I'd never try and take Susu from you. Don't you believe me?"

"Yes, but hell, you're her mother." His frown deepened, but now she saw a glint in his eyes. "And I'm her father. Now what could we possibly do to see to it that each of us plays an equal role in our little girl's life?"

All at once she was afraid to breathe. "I don't know," she whispered. "Did you have something in mind?"

Roarke nodded. "Marry me, Toria. Be my wife, as well as Susanna's mother." He kissed her again, more deeply than before. "And let me take care of both of you forever."

A warm summer breeze came in the open window over the pansies' soft velvet petals. Victoria saw their heads dip, as if in obeisance, and all at once her heart swelled with joy.

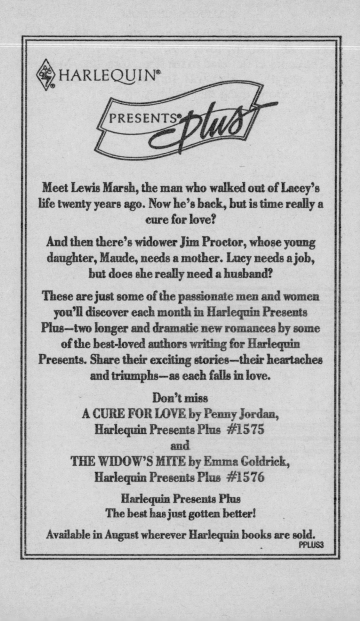

"Yes," she said, looping her arms around Roarke's neck, "oh, yes, my love. Yes."

The contract fluttered to the floor, forgotten. Moments later everything else was forgotten, too—everything except the one thing that endures.

Love.

HARLEQUIN PRESENTS®

A Year
DOWN UNDER

In 1993, Harlequin Presents celebrates the land down
under. In August let us take you to Auckland and
Northland, New Zealand, in THE STONE PRINCESS by
Robyn Donald, Harlequin Presents #1577.

They'd parted eight years ago, but Petra still feels
something for Caine Fleming. Now the handsome New
Zealander wants to reconcile, but Petra isn't convinced of
his true feelings for her. She does know that she wants—
that she *needs*—any reconciliation to be more than a
marriage of convenience. Petra wants Caine body and soul.

Share the adventure—and the romance—of
A Year Down Under!

Available this month in
A Year Down Under

NO RISKS, NO PRIZES
by Emma Darcy
Harlequin Presents #1570
Available wherever Harlequin books are sold.

YDU-JL